Praise for

The Calypso Chronicles

★ "Not far behind the giddy, ultra-glitzy fun lurks
a generous spirit. Bring on the sequel."
—*Publishers Weekly* on *Pulling Princes*, starred review

"[An] endearing and energetic exposé of English boarding-school life. . . .
Sharp, honest, and seriously entertaining, making this an enjoyable read,
and crowning O'Connell the latest British teen queen."
—*Kirkus Reviews* on *Pulling Princes*

"Give this to fans of Princess Mia and Georgia Nicholson."
—*Booklist* on *Stealing Princes*

"There is never a dull moment in this boarding school. . . . Calypso is
an engaging character who evokes sympathy and provides plenty
laugh-out-loud moments." —*VOYA* on *Stealing Princes*

"O'Connell's Calypso Chronicles blend appealing components of such
popular series as Gossip Girls and The Princess Diaries. In this install-
ment, Calypso is at the top of her game." —*Booklist* on *Dueling Princes*

"While some girl series only have designer clothes and city settings to
keep them going, Calypso's adventures have enough facets to keep
readers on both sides of the Atlantic coming back for more."
—TeenReads.com on *Dumping Princes*

"The novel gallops forward at a rollicking pace. With a liberal serving
of engaging characters, slapstick comedy, and a fabulous boarding-school
setting, *Dumping Princes* is the best in the series so far. It is sure to have
fans of the previous novels rolling on the floor laughing their royal
crowns off." —*SLJ* on *Dumping Princes*

Not every frog who wears a crown
turns out to be a prince . . .

Books by Tyne O'Connell

The Calypso Chronicles:

Pulling Princes

Stealing Princes

Dueling Princes

Dumping Princes

True Love, the Sphinx, and Other Unsolvable Riddles

Dumping Princes

THE CALYPSO CHRONICLES

by Tyne O'Connell

BLOOMSBURY

To my muses, Her Royal Magnifiqueness,
the stylish Cordelia O'Connell,
and my worshipfully clever Santospirito sons,
Zad and Kajj, who brought Italy and Windsor
to life for me.

Copyright © 2006 by Tyne O'Connell
First published by Bloomsbury U.S.A. Children's Books in 2006
Paperback edition published in 2007

Published by Bloomsbury U.S.A. Children's Books
175 Fifth Avenue, New York, NY 10010
Distributed to the trade by Holtzbrinck Publishers

The Library of Congress has cataloged the hardcover edition as follows:
O'Connell, Tyne.
Dumping princes / by Tyne O'Connell.—1st U.S. ed.
p.   cm. (The Calypso chronicles)
Summary: When Prince Freddie breaks up with her, Calypso—with the help of her entire
school—tries to win him back in order to perform a "counter dump."
ISBN-13: 978-1-58234-852-0 • ISBN-10: 1-58234-852-9 (hardcover)
[1. Interpersonal relations—Fiction. 2. Princes—Fiction. 3. Boarding schools—Fiction.
4. Schools—Fiction. 5. England—Fiction. 6. Humorous stories.]
I. Title. II. Series: O'Connell, Tyne. Calypso chronicles.
PZ7.O2168Dum 2006   [Fic]—dc22   2005035502

ISBN-13: 978-1-59990-150-3 • ISBN-10: 1-59990-150-1 (paperback)

Typeset by Hewer Text UK Ltd, Edinburgh
Printed in the U.S.A. by Quebecor World Fairfield
1 3 5 7 9 10 8 6 4 2

Acknowledgements

First up, shout outs to the stunning, preternaturally gifted girls of Saint Mary's Ascot, Cheltenham Ladies College, Bennerz and my favourite Etonians, you know, the really, really fit ones! In fact, the entire boarding school community should take a bow! I hope your teachers, masters, matrons, bursars and house mothers applaud you every day because one day you'll be in a position to hand out the blues! Speaking of blue, I would be dismally blue without the friendship of Malcolm William Young. In fact, if he didn't exist, I'd have to make him up.

I totally lucked out having an agent like Laura Dail and an editor like Melanie Cecka at Bloomsbury USA. And I know it! Every day I do a mad little tribute dance in their honour. So far, only my family have seen my mad-dance. They recommend I hold off a few millennia before unleashing it on a wider audience. Until that day, I salute you in Latin, *Salve*!

But the laurels and really, really worshipful words go to the girls who read my books, especially the girls who write in to askcalypso@calypsochronicles.com. Seriously, if you don't grow up and rule the world, and see your names in lights over Times Square, I shall unleash my mad little dance.

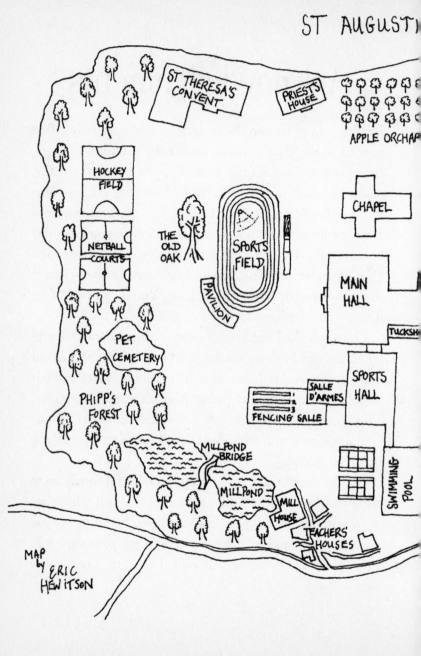

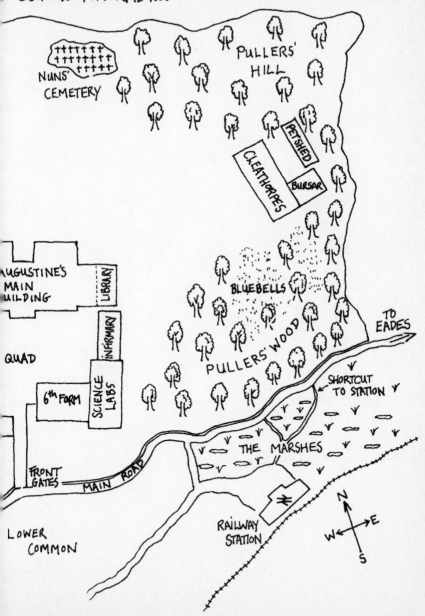

ONE

Sound the Alert! Americans Are Storming the Castle!

According to my darling 'rentals, I lack a sense of proportion. Oh, and I thrive on melodrama.

They base this on something that happened in the Beverly Centre shopping mall when I was three years old, which was henceforth referred to as 'The Incident.'

Whenever the 'rents want to back up their claims of my lack of proportion and need for drama, they mention The Incident. Allegedly, it involved a Christmas tree, a pair of black lace knickers and a police report.

The padre usually adds something daft like, 'One day you'll go too far, Calypso Kelly.' To which my madre will nod sagely and say, 'All right, well, I think we've made our point. Let's not go *there* again.'

The mad 'rents, who insist I call them Sarah and Bob, are not going to win any prizes for their own sense of proportion or lack of drama. And as for going *too far*, well, they crossed that line years ago when they named me Calypso and packed me off to boarding school in England so I wouldn't become 'too Hollywood' – whatever that means.

No, Sarah and Bob are the very apex of dramarama. They tell lies. Yes, whopping great porkies – and I'm not just talking about the alleged Incident in the mall or the Tooth Fairy. They also told me I was the cleverest, prettiest, most talented girl in all the world. That's what I mean. They're sweet, but daft as socks.

Anyway, on this particular day, I was over the moon-arama for an indisputably good reason! I was off to stay with Their Royal Majesties. But every silver lining has a cloud: my parents were driving me and staying for lunch-eon.

Absolutely nothing was going to spoil my excitement over going to visit my fit prince in his Scottish castle, that enormous grey stony one with the fairy-tale turrets, where kilt-ish carryons such as reeling, haggis eating, grouse shooting and jigs like the Gay Gordons are *de rigueur*. They often show the royal family standing outside their castle on television and in magazines. It is très, très divine.

All I had to say to anyone who doubted our love would last was, eat your knickers. I was still – pinch yourselves – pulling Prince Freddie, as regularly as I reasonably could. I mean, heirs to the throne do spend a lot of time in training to be king, which was tedious. But I never complained.

No, I was determined not to be a tragic, clingy-type girlfriend. My wildly independent American streak still thrived!

You'd think any normal parents might be proud that their daughter was dating the heir to the crown, but no, no, no, no, no. That would be too sensible for Bob and Sarah. 'You don't think you're being a bit melodramatic about this relationship with Freddie, do you, Calypso?' Bob suggested as we hit the M1 motorway. 'I mean, you've only just turned fifteen last week and you're acting like you're going to marry the boy.'

I turned up the volume on my iPod and started humming loudly to a particularly tuneless and depressing song which my best friend, Star, wrote. It's called 'The Only Guarantee in Life Is School Sucks.'

I think she got the idea for the song from our three-thousand-year-old religious studies teacher, Sister Bethlehem. She's always banging on about how there are no guarantees in life, which is a blatant lie, because you can always guarantee that Sister Bethlehem will fall asleep in class. Mind you, there are certain Old Testament books that send me off into a good snooze. Like Leviticus.

Even so, I am feverishly fond of old Sister Bethlehem. She is always teaching us useful life skills, like how to win money by betting on things – such as who cut off Samson's hair in the Bible.

'Yes, girls, you can win quite a tidy sum of money on that one,' she told us once. 'A lot of people will tell you it was Delilah, but if they bothered to read the Good Book more closely, they'd realise she actually called for a servant to lop off his locks. Mark my words, if you're ever short of a pound, that one will come in very handy. I won a fiver off Father Conway two years on the trot with that one.'

But back to guarantees. I could guarantee I would never, never, never tire of Freddie's lips. So don't start running a book on that because you will lose. The 'rentals call it puppy love, but then again, they *are* absurdly old and quite, quite foolish.

Freds didn't seem keen for me to visit him in his palatial grandeur initially. I can't think why, after I exposed him to the lunacy of Sarah and Bob. But eventually, after aggressive hinting on my part (what is it with boys that they can't take hints?), he caved and invited me to stay the weekend at Harthnoon Castle. I guess he finally realised that if he kept me and his Kiltland retreat apart for much longer, I would start growing paws from all my shameless begging.

It was all quite surreal being invited to stay with the Royal Family. Like the rest of the world, I'd seen Freds and his family in their mad kilts doing photo calls outside Harthnoon Castle. But like every other girl who has drooled over this fit prince, I never imagined in my maddest of mad dreams that I'd ever actually be invited to stay with him there. Okay, so maybe in my maddest dreams . . . but then, what girl my age hasn't? Freds was the object of desire for teenage girls worldwide.

Apart from my best friend, Star, that is.

Star thought he was 'an arrogant, boring, unworthy drip with bad taste in clothes.' Oh, and did I mention, seriously unworthy of *moi*? Then again, Star didn't think any boy was good enough for any girl. Not because she's from the Isle of Lesbos or anything, it's just that she had a much higher opinion of girls than of boys. But then if you met her father, Tiger, from the legendary rock band Dirge, you'd understand why. It's a wonder she isn't deeply unhinged.

Love her though I do, her snide comments about how "stuck up" Freds was were becoming très, très, très annoying. He couldn't be that stuck up if he loved an American Freak like me, could he? Well, that's what my psycho toff anti-girlfriend Honey said, anyway. It's hardly ideal when I have to cite something the poisonous Honey has said to defend something as fundamental as my love for Freddie.

Star had been ultra horrible about Freds, especially after she dumped his best friend, Kev. Oh yes, that's my latest news flash. Hold onto your knickers – my best friend had gone over to the mad side. After she dumped Kev, she started on this loony mission to get *me* to dump *Freds*, which was as maddening as a drawer of tangled tights.

My fainting attacks began when she dumped Kev. 'You what?' I asked as she brought me around, using the age-old tickling method. Kev was Fred's best friend, and the symmetry of *my* best friend hanging out with *his* best friend was a vital element in the joy of loving Freds. She couldn't dump Kev! She couldn't. 'You can't dump Kev,' I told her.

'Well, I did,' said Star. 'I told you I wanted to start the year with a clean slate, darling,' she reminded me, referring to the New Year resolutions we'd made together in her bedroom wing while her parents and their celebrity friends rock-and-rolled the night away.

My resolutions were the normal unrealistic goals of a teenage girl; stop picking at my spots and develop more savoir-faire and va-va-va-voom. To that end, I was going to start littering my sentences with loads of foreign words and *bon mots*. I was also harbouring deep hopes of doing well in my GCSE exams and wowing them with my fencing prowess in Italy, where I would be participating in my first international tournament. I'd had a letter about the Italian trip over the break, but with Christmas, my birthday and my parents' constant canoodling, I hadn't had a chance to get properly excited about it. Especially as Freds wasn't on the national team, which meant even more time I wouldn't get to spend with him.

'I thought you meant stuff like, erm, taking those blue extensions out of your hair and perfecting your French accent,' I told her. 'Not dumping perfectly good boyfriends!'

Star scoffed. 'Calypso, don't you ever wonder if there's more to life than boys?'

'No!' I blurted. 'I mean, of course I wonder that all the time.'

'We're still young, darling. Don't you think we should be focusing on our dreams rather than spotty boys?'

I decided not to say anything lame about how Freds *was* my dream – well, my dream boyfriend anyway. But he is. And he is not in the least bit spotty!

And then in the car driving up to Kiltland, the padre said much the same thing. 'I know you want to impress Freds and his folks, but don't you think taking a trunk of outfits for a weekend stay is a bit over the top?'

'You really have no idea, Bob,' I told him, and then I brooded about whether he was right. I mean, I didn't want Freds or the king and queen to think I was desperate to impress. Even if I was.

TWO

The Collision of Parental Culture Shock

As the 'rents drove our car of shame up to the castle, we had to pass a large crowd of royal watchers. I call it the car of shame not *just* because it's not a chauffeur-driven Rolls Royce like all my other friends' cars. No, it has a bumper sticker that reads – this is true, by the way – HONK IF YOU'RE IN LURVE!

Très, très mortifying.

The fans were keeping vigil in the rain in the hope of spotting their beloved royals. Quite a few of them were holding placards with WE LOVE YOU PRINCE FREDDIE! printed on them. I had to give quite a few death stares to the more brazen girls whose signs promised all sorts of indecent pleasures to my lovely Freds.

Bob and Sarah, on the other hand, felt compelled to give the hussies a little wave as security ushered us through. My 'rentals are soooo delusional. It was as if they thought *they* were royalty or something.

I would have ducked down on the floor of the car of shame if I wasn't so afraid of ruining my outfit, which was too feverishly stunning for words. Unfortunately, Freds had seen it before, because my cruel padre had refused to hand over his precious plastic. 'You don't ever give a boy the idea you care too much' was his excuse.

To ensure I'd fit in amongst the royals at Harthnoon Castle, I'd been practising my regal walk over Christmas. I wished I wasn't so freakishly tall, though. I know I prayed for a growth spurt a few years back, but honestly, it was getting ridiculous. I was seriously worried my long blond-ish locks would get caught up in low-hanging chandeliers.

Freds told me that he loves everything about me, but I'm sure I've grown ten feet since he last saw me two weeks ago. It would be a great test of his love if he could still care for me once I started swinging from his family's chandelier by my hair during afternoon tea.

As someone wonderfully good and great in the Bible, or another heavy book, once remarked, 'so many problems, so few solutions.' Or maybe that was, 'so many people, so few fish'? I was cramming so much knowledge into my brain for my GCSEs at the moment, my head was about to explode. That would teach the examination board a lesson or two.

Everyone knows how divinely fit and marvellous my prince is, so I won't bang on too much about His Royal Handsomeness. I'll just mention that in the beginning, I had to pinch myself that I, Calypso Kelly, onetime Queen of the School Losers Association at the toffer-than-thou English girls' boarding school I attend, was pulling a prince. All the other girls at Saint Augustine's live in a world of total freedom, Daddy's plastic, mummy's contacts, personal manservants, chauffer-driven Rolls Royces, bodyguards, society pages and titles that go back hundreds of years. Whereas I have a family that can trace itself back to Kentucky, Sarah and Bob, a car of shame, curfew rules and a fixed allowance.

Then again, I was the one going out with the prince.

Sometimes I even pinched myself when I was kissing him and screamed out: 'Ouch!' Freds found that a trifle weird. Mind you, he found a lot of things about me peculiar. But he was perfection itself, and I honestly couldn't imagine ever breaking up with him.

Okay, so there *was* one teensy weensy fly in the ointment of our perfect love, and when I say teensy weensy, I mean smaller than an iota, so strictly speaking it's not even visible under a microscope. The scoop is . . . he's pretty, erm, normal, really.

Yes, normal, as in just like a regular non-royal-type person. Not a bit mad or even mildly eccentric in the least. But that's a good thing, right?

Well, you try telling Star that!

I know what you're thinking, he's a prince, he can't be boring. But it's true, the most shocking secret about the royals is just how boringly, boringly ordinary they are. And I say that with the utmost love and respect. Seriously, not only do they wander about the palace without their crowns and magisterial robes on, they do things like eat toast for breakfast! Ordinary old toast! Can you believe it? I couldn't.

When Freds first told me this shocking news regarding his family's penchant for toast, I had to grip onto him to stop fainting. I imagined they'd eat special royal-type food specially developed by royal scientists and organic health experts. But no, they ate normal food, chatted away about the weather and watched television like everyone else. And, oh my giddy aunt . . . they don't even have cable!

I would die without cable.

The one *slight* worry I had on receiving my invite to Harthnoon was how to get out of shooting things. Freds and his family love nothing better than a good shoot at the expense of some poor creature. I'm not a big fan of shooting things, as Freds knows perfectly well. But I figured I was on display, so I had to devise a cunning plan to escape the shoot without upsetting the symmetry of this longed-for weekend.

Star warned me that if I told his family I didn't like killing things, they would think me freakish. I feared they thought me freakish anyway after my 'rentals, Sarah and Bob, tongue-kissed one another when they dropped me off in Scotland around noon. What if the king and queen were soooo normal they did things like peer out the curtains? I thought. *Quelle horreur!*

Am I wrong to wish that Bob and Sarah wouldn't

tongue-kiss in public? They thought I should be pleased that they were back together after their six-week separation last term. I *was* pleased. Of course I was pleased. They were hopeless without one another. All I was asking was that they stop slobbering over each other all the time.

Of course that's exactly what they did on our arrival – kiss. What if the tabloids got a shot of my parents kissing like teenagers at the castle?

'Stop that, you two,' I scolded. 'What will the royal family think of you?'

'Chill out, Calypso, they're just people like us,' Bob said.

'Just people!' I squawked like a madder-than-mad thing. 'Like us?'

Even the liveried footman, who was getting my trunk out of the boot, looked shocked. I was close to certain that the king and queen *don't* pull in public – if they even pull at all.

'Heck, do we tip this guy or what?' asked Bob, pulling out his wallet. He actually talks like that too. Words like 'gee,' 'swell' and 'hip' litter his every sentence. When I was younger and more vulnerable, I used to walk on the other side of the street from him or sit in a different booth in diners. I'm a lot stronger now.

'Erm, no,' I told him with the authority of a person who gets her information on the royal family from Google. 'Just give me some cash,' I said firmly, wrestling with his wallet. 'You're meant to leave your tip *after* your stay.' Well, that is the deal for country house stays – according to www.englisheysnobs.com – and this was sort of like a country house, just a really, really big one with turrets and a moat.

'But *we're* not staying,' Sarah pointed out reasonably enough. 'We're heading off for our romantic weekend after luncheon.'

I wished they'd stop banging on about their 'romantic' weekend. I really didn't want to imagine what they planned to get up to.

'No, but I'm staying,' I hissed, not wanting the lurking footman to hear. 'So give it to me.' I tugged the wallet out of Bob's hand, deftly relieving it of a bunch of readies.

Bob gave me one of his "one day you'll go too far, Calypso Kelly" looks, but Freds had come out by that point, so Bob didn't say anything. I know this sounds shallow and culturally small-minded, but I was quite pleased that Freds wasn't wearing a kilt. Not that I don't love a kilt on a boy, it's just, well, it makes me feel like grabbing his arm and doing the Gay Gordons or some other loony reel.

But Freds was sans kilt and his black hair was doing that wildly wonderful sticky-outy thing I loved so much. His eyes looked bluer than blue too in the Scottish air. It was a crisp, bright day, and he looked soooo fit in his regulation navy blue Ralph Lauren thin knit jumper over pale blue Ralph Lauren shirt, neutral-coloured trousers and some sort of hiking-type boot, which my mother pointed out. Trust Sarah. The boy is a god and all she could say was, 'See how sensible his shoes are, Calypso?'

Seeing Freds resplendent in all his worshipful beauty, I was glad I'd pulled out all the stops on my own outfit. I was wearing no makeup (apart from six inches of lip-gloss and lashings of mascara), because boys really go for the natural look. I had also splurged on a new brown corduroy mini-skirt from Top Shop, and the green cashmere jumper Star had given me for Christmas matched my green sequined slippers perfectly. To think that Sarah had actually tried to make me change into Wellington boots before we left! Yes, Wellington boots.

'Believe me, his parents will respect you for it,' she'd said as I was dressing to leave. 'Scotland can be very wet and boggy.'

I didn't even know what boggy was, but I'm sure the royals don't muck about in it. So hoping to silence Sarah with my royal knowledge, I asked, 'Who thinks Wellington boots are suitable footwear for lunch with the royal family?' I asked, and then I said, 'Mr and Mrs No One. That's who.'

You'd think that would have silenced the mad madre, but no, she went on and on for another ten million years about the virtues of Wellington boots over sequined slippers. I have no idea how she ever pulled Bob if her idea of seductive footwear is a pair of rubber boots.

To tell the truth, I don't want to know.

I pretended to faint just to shut her up, only coming to when it was time to get in the car. My new swooning/fainting strategy had proved an invaluable weapon in this war against parental insanity.

My parents had been invited to "take luncheon with Their Majesties," which sounds madly grand, but as it turned out, luncheon consisted only of nasty cold meats, a selection of peculiar cheeses that smelt like a hiker's sweaty socks and some horrible old red wine.

Bob and Sarah seemed totally at home with Queen Adelaide and King Alfred. And being Bob and Sarah, they were calling them Addie and Al by the time they left. I was mouthing 'don't' and waving my hands to stop them all through lunch, but they refused to acknowledge me. Apart from Bob, who mouthed 'paranoid' back at me.

As I stood beside Freds to wave them good-bye, they kissed one another *again*. I decided that was soooo going to be the last time I took them to meet a boyfriend's parents. Not that I planned on having another boyfriend or anything. No, Freds was the perfect boyfriend for me. Although I wouldn't mind if he grew a few more inches.

THREE

The Most
Spectacular Fib

Actually, Freds' parents had taken a shine to Bob and Sarah. Me, on the other hand? Well, apparently they thought I was 'sickly and sniffly.' Okay, so I had forced Freds to tell me what they thought of me. I just think he could have put it a tad more kindly.

'I think it was the runny nose,' Freds added, by means of explanation.

Oh yes, my cold. My genius excuse for not going on the shoot the following day. It was really a most spectacularly elaborate fib. I'd even gone to the trouble of cunningly rubbing a handkerchief with chili oil to produce the glassy-eyed, runny nose effect. It was a tip I'd picked up at Saint Augustine's to get out of a class.

So, while the royals were off killing things, I sat in the library (just like at Saint Augustine's only sans computers). Freds' twinkly-eyed gran sat with me. She was quite sweet and very merry, knocking back sherry after sherry and prank calling the staff. We got on quite well in a drunken old duck/sober teenager sort of way. Unfortunately her two old Labradors kept nipping me. 'That's their way of saying hello, don't you know,' Gran had explained as they gnawed my legs off.

Sarah's parents had died in a car accident when I was small, and Bob's parents lived in Kentucky, so I barely ever saw them. When I did, they obsessed about my milk intake, like I was some sort of calf or something. Freds' gran, on the other hand, made me try a glass of sherry, which tastes like cough mixture. I think I may have got a bit tipsy, because I started calling her Bea instead of Ma'am. Also, I let Bea use my mobile to call the butler, who was refusing to answer her calls on the house phones after numerous pranks informing him of all sorts of scandalous untruths about what he got up to in his free time. Honestly, she was soooo funny I chortled my knickers off.

I was still chortling away like the Laughing Cavalier in that famous painting that hangs in the Wallace Collection when Freds and his 'rents came back from killing innocent creatures. The Laughing Cavalier in the painting doesn't look like he's laughing – he looks like he's grinning in a knowing, pervy way if you ask me.

So I suppose that didn't look too good.

Freds gave me a disappointed look as we all gathered in the drawing room, which looked out onto a lovely loch. I was peering out in the hope of seeing a monster or something fascinating like that when the queen asked, 'How's your cold, Calypso?'

'My what?' I replied, having completely forgotten my elaborate ruse.

'Your cold?' Freddie reminded me – a bit sternly.

'Oh, that.' I produced my handkerchief and took a deep sniff, which set me off coughing, which in turn set the Labradors off on another nipping attack on my legs. 'A little better, I think.'

'Oh marvellous,' the king replied, slapping the arms of his chair with delight. 'We wouldn't want you to miss your mother's marvellous show because of illness.' Honestly, Freds' 'rents were as bonkeresque as mine. First toast and now this!

I'd love to have missed Sarah's 'marvellous' show. I think Freds knew that, because he gave me one of his cautioning looks, which were becoming far too regular for my liking.

'No, no, I can't get enough of *Harley Village*,' I told them with a great deal of feeling. I was getting scarily good at this lying thing.

Harley Village is *the* most agonisingly dreary dramarama about a village in Yorkshire where a missing pig is front-page news. It had been Britain's highest-rated series for fifty years or something, and Sarah was sadly proud to have this new gig. I don't know why she couldn't have kept up her morning celebrity slot. The boys at Eades adored the madre's morning show – which of course meant kudos for me.

Sarah could talk about how atmospheric *Harley Village*

is until the cows came home, but as far as I was concerned, it was a show about miserable wet people arguing over whose umbrella was whose.

'Splendid,' said the king.

'Excellent,' agreed the queen.

'Bollocks,' blurted Bea. For a micro-moment, I actually thought the exclamation had come from me. Then Bea winked at me, and I had to snort so deeply into my handkerchief to smother my laughter, I almost passed out.

That was the worst thing about the weekend: my fake cold. Once I'd faked the cold to avoid the shoot, I couldn't exactly make a miraculous recovery without everyone becoming suspicious. It was merde! I had to sniffle and cough all weekend. And as it turned out, my cold was totally pointless.

As I was having my good-bye kiss alone with Freds in one of the turreted towers that smelt of moss, I naively confided in him about how and why I'd lied about having a cold. He knew how much I hated shooting animals, so I thought he'd understand. Actually, I had hoped he'd laugh like a mad thing and spin me around in his arms, but all he did was give me another one of his disappointed looks. I hated his disappointed looks. Every time he gave me one, I felt myself becoming dimmer in his eyes. Then he said, 'It was a *clay* pigeon shoot, Calypso. I am perfectly aware how *anti* you are.'

I don't know how he does it, but he manages to make my dislike of murdering animals sound like treason.

Is it my fault no one ever tells me anything? Buggery boyfriends and their stupid expectations and disappointed looks. It wasn't easy sniffing on that chili-soaked handkerchief all weekend. But did he give me any thanks, or any respect, or encouragement? No.

Now his parents thought I was sickly and sniffly and they would probably banish me from all their castles forever, and Freds and I would be confined to cafés and pizza shops like ordinary girls and boys. Merde, merde and double algebra merde.

Basically, the weekend was not the triumph I had hoped it would be, and I returned to London in a major sulk. The icing on the cake was that my green bejewelled slippers got all soggy when Freds took me walking in some bogs. 'You should have worn Wellingtons,' he told me.

And then just when I thought life couldn't get any worse, I ended up with a really nasty cold.

FOUR

Witness to Madness

I left the castle feeling less than magical.

When I arrived back at the house my parents were renting in Clapham, London – The Clap House, as my evil anti-girlfriend Honey O'Hare had named it – my life took another nosedive.

Sarah and Bob pitched up to my bedroom, swung open the door (without so much as a courteous knock) and declared in one voice, 'We have decided to get married, Calypso.'

All I said was, 'Fine,' because, well, the 'rents are always lobbing up and saying the most random things.

I was listening to my favourite song on the really cool green iPod they'd given me for my combined birthday/Christmas present. Oh, and txting Freds at the same time because some ancient Greek chap in a toga (or was it a bath?) once said, 'Life is too short to limit oneself to one activity at a time.' Then again, I might have read that in a fortune cookie.

However, my parents' announcement slowly began to

seep into my consciousness, and I pressed Send before I'd even added any x's. I turned around to face them, ripped my earphones out of my ears and stated the blindingly obvious. 'But you *are* married!'

They giggled like loons.

And then a horrible idea occurred to me. 'You've not been buying things off hooded men on the Landor Road?' I asked sternly, because the last thing I needed was my mad parents to start smoking weed and end up like Star's father, Tiger. Yes, he was probably in a semi-vegetative state on his kitchen floor even at that moment. Star claimed the reason he called everyone 'man' was because he had no memory cells left. It must be très, très mortifying having a father like Tiger.

Bob and Sarah have never shown an interest in exploring drug culture, but they are extremely gullible, especially Bob. Honestly, since coming to London in December he's been mugged like nine times. That's more than once a week. No matter how many times I tell him not to pull his entire wallet out when he wants to give a pound to a beggar at a crowded tube station, he persists in doing it. Proving that parents need round-the-clock supervision. I really don't know how they'll cope once I grow up.

Bob and Sarah looked into one another's eyes and laughed. They had been doing that a lot since they got back together, which is why I'd been forced into this unwanted role as a sensible parent-type person rather than the irresponsible adolescent I *should* have been.

'No, Calypso, we're not smoking weeeeed,' they reassured me. 'It's just that we've never been married in England,' Sarah explained.

'You haven't been married in Mississippi either, Sarah; that's not the point,' I told the mad madre calmly. 'You can't just go round the world marrying one another. It's probably not even legal.'

'Why not?' Bob asked, giving my mother's bottom a playful pinch, which made her squeal.

'It's called bigamy, Bob,' I told him, even though I don't know if marrying the same person over and over *is* called bigamy. But I do know it is madness. They didn't listen, though. I watched my giggling 'rents for a bit longer as they tickled and kissed in my doorway.

In the face of such parental madness, I put my earphones back in and said, 'Fine,' with the dismissive tone that any teenager whose parents have just fallen back in love will be only too familiar with.

There was no talking them out of it, either. During the last week of the Christmas holidays, Bob and Sarah had had a marriage blessing in Windsor Chapel. And that's another thing. Of all the picturesque places to wed, they chose the one a few steps from one of Freddie's family castles. When I begged them to choose another lovely church, they rolled their eyes and said I was being 'paranoid.' They've been saying that a lot lately. Luckily Freds and his 'rents were still up in their Kiltland castle.

Bob's parents, affectionately known as The Gams, came

out for the blessing and gave me twenty dollars worth of book vouchers from their local bookstore in Kentucky.

I've never even been to Kentucky, so I don't know what they could have been thinking.

After the 'wedding,' which was really only a blessing, Bob and Sarah threw a big party back at the Clap House. It's actually a really lovely house, and Sarah and Bob invited all my friends to the reception and said they could sleep over, which made me feel more supportive of their madness. But then Sarah and Bob spoilt everything by a very public, very passionate kiss as they cut the cake. It lasted – this is true, by the way – forty-nine painfully embarrassing seconds. I timed it on my mobile while all my friends took photos of them with their camera phones.

I was witnessing insanity in its truest form.

'They're soooo cute,' Star squealed as she took photo after photo of the cute couple snog-aging.

FIVE

H to the O to the N to the E to the Y

The kissing didn't stop after the wedding/blessing affair, either. They were still doing it when they took me back for my first day of term. I had been really looking forward to being dropped off at school by my parents too. This was the first time in years that I didn't have to make my own way to Saint Augustine's from the airport after the LAX-to-Heathrow hell flight.

It was a festival of luxury being driven back to school by the 'rents, even if it was in a car of shame which neither of them could drive properly. The biggest advantage to having Sarah and Bob drive me to school was they could help carry my madly heavy trunk and fencing kit up the stairs to the dorms just like all the other girls' parents and valets. Hoorah! Well . . . that was the plan I'd hatched in Calypso's Very Own Fantasyland at least.

My school is an odd little world within an odd little world. For an American, it's sort of like a culture shock within a culture shock. Sarah sent me to this school because she was born in England and she went here – and loved it. I never thought I would love it, but after four years of being the school misfit, I had actually started to get into the swing of it. But maybe that's because I'm more or less into the swing of being a misfit too.

As we drove down the fern-lined track to the entrance of Saint Augustine's, we passed small groups of tiny little nuns wandering along holding hands. They all waved at us, and Bob tooted the horn. The nuns are soooo sweet. They never punish us or roll their eyes at us like other grown-ups. Also, they sneak us into their convent sometimes for little tea parties and ply us with sweets and Battenberg cake.

As we parked the car of shame alongside the Bentleys, Range Rovers and Rolls Royces, Bob and Sarah declared they'd better not carry more than the trunk.

'We wouldn't want to put our backs out,' Bob said.

'Never mind that my vertebrae have been cracking under the strain for years!' I muttered.

It was agreed that I would lug the shoulder-cutting fencing kit, my hand luggage and my rabbit, Dorothy Parker. Not that I'm *totally* complaining. I love carrying Dorothy (especially in her new lime green leather carrier). I don't trust anyone with my fencing kit, and I definitely didn't want Sarah and Bob near my hand luggage, as it contained my Body Shop Specials – aka vodka. Also, the trunk weighed like five thousand pounds!

The problems only arose when, halfway up, they attempted another kiss. Obviously they'd never studied basic physics, because by taking their hands off the trunk it went belting down the narrow winding stairs, knocking a gaggle of parents, valets and other girls flying in the process.

I was struggling with my own load some way behind them when one of the girls they'd knocked fell back into me, and I was sent sprawling in a heap on the stone floor at the foot of the stairs. Neither Bob nor Sarah bothered to see if I was okay. I don't think they'd even registered the disaster their snog-aging had caused.

I was just checking Dorothy when the Not So Honourable Honey O'Hare and her horrible manservant, Oopa, followed by some random guy in orange Buddhist robes, stepped over me as if I were roadkill.

Honey addressed me in that special psycho-toff sneering way she has perfected over a zillion put-downs. 'Oh, the American refugee has returned. I thought the new immigration regulations would have seen you off.' Then she pursed her collagen-enhanced lips and laughed hyena-like at her own wit. Between her Botox and her collagen implants, her face was pulled in all directions. It was not a pretty sight.

Oopa just stood wheezing evilly by her side. His spine was probably breaking under the weight of Honey's LVT steamer trunk and custom-made LVT luggage, but I was soooo over feeling sorry for Oopa after the way he had reacted the last time I offered to help him. The Buddhist monk guy was looking peacefully into the middle distance.

I didn't respond to Honey's attack. It's a survival skill I picked up over my four years at Saint Augustine's. I had faced my fear-of-fears last term when I shared a room with her, but I wasn't sharing a bedroom with her this term, so our *froidure* was back on. My *modus operandi* was to have as little to do with her as possible.

Honey wasn't finished with *me* though. She opened her mouth as if about to launch into one of her 'H to the O to the N to the E to the Y' rants. Then she looked up and stopped.

I followed her gaze and saw what had captured her attention. Bob and Sarah were standing under the stained glass window of Mary and the infant Jesus, wearing the same look of rapt adoration for one another they'd been sporting all holiday – and giggling.

'That,' Honey sneered, pointing at Bob and Sarah with one of her evil talons, 'is the most revolting sight I have ever endured.' Then she did her signature shiver of disgust before taking a deep breath and setting off up the stairs followed by her manservant and the Buddhist monk–type chap.

If she hadn't been Honey, I would have agreed with her. Instead I silently gathered my rabbit and kit together and followed her as imperiously as I could. Like most of the girls and parents, she was tanned from her New Year ski trip to Val d'Isere. But unlike them, she was wearing the most revealing yellow sundress and gold Jimmy Choo strappy sandals. Of course, she was also wearing those other two never-be-seen-without Sloane accessories: the implausibly small bejewelled phone (permanently glued to ear) and a five-hundred-dollar pash wrapped around her neck like an African tribal choker.

Halfway up, Honey turned and ran her eyes up and down me like an evil prison guard's searchlight. Under her scrutiny, I looked down at my unremarkable outfit to see what the problem was. I even checked the soles of my dilapidated green bejewelled slippers as I waited for her attack.

Eventually she said, 'Well?'

So I said, 'Well what?'

'Your chavscum parents are blocking the stairwell, you American Freak.'

I craned my neck and saw she was right. Oh my giddy aunt, it was unbelievable. They were *still* canoodling, completely oblivious to all the people who were struggling to squeeze past them. I called out sharply, 'Sarah and Bob! Stop that at once!'

You can see how badly this role reversal was affecting me.

SIX

Bohemian Rhapsody in the Dorm

This term I was rooming with two of my first choices: boy-crazed, adorably sentimental Clementine and a princess from Nigeria, Indiamacca – known as Clems and Indie, respectively. Both girls were already in the room chatting on their tiny phones – Indie's phone is soooo feverishly cool. It is purple enamel and has her name picked out in *real* diamonds.

Clems' parents and my parents were chatting together as they unpacked our clothes. Clems' little brother Sebastian was opening and shutting the wardrobe door, pretending to be a savage animal and biting the clothes as they were being placed inside by the grown-ups. He was three now and looking less and less like a Jelly Baby and more and more like a bad elf.

Indie's valet was unpacking for his mistress, while her security guards were decorating the room in her trademark purple.

I was so used to the madness of my school life in England now that I barely gave a second glance to the two burly suits in buzz cuts balanced on dainty floral stools as they hung the purple curtains.

I hadn't seen Indie or Clemmie since last term, so I was far more desperate to hear their goss. But before the hugs and air-kisses were over, I overheard Sarah say to Clemmie's parents (and anyone else with hearing in the building), 'Yes, we got married at Christmas. It was soooo romantic.'

Seriously, this was atrocious. I was sure Indie's valet and security men couldn't care less about Bob and Sarah's marital unions. But Clemmie's parents were another matter. Clems' 'rents were not bohemian rhapsodies like Star's or mine. No, they were your normal, madly conservative, Tory-voting 'rentals.

This was an emergency. Acting on instinct, I dove over Indie's valet, who was carefully placing designer casuals in the drawer under her bed, clamped my hand over Sarah's mouth, and cried out, 'Stop saying that!' Turning to Clems' 'rents, I explained, 'Honestly, they were married years before I was born! It was just a repeat performance. I don't want any trouble.'

Mr and Mrs Fraser Marks looked at me as if I were a mad adolescent on hormonal meltdown. Then Clems' madre spoke directly to Sarah. 'Yes, Clementine told us about the blessing. Congratulations to you both.'

I removed my hand from Sarah's mouth and pretended

that I had merely been brushing her face for crumbs. Sarah shook her head and frowned, so I planted a dutiful-daughter kiss on her nose.

Bob gave me one of his "you're so paranoid, Calypso" glares. I slunk back over to Indie and Clemmie. Stupid, stupid, stupid Calypso – I wish I'd fainted instead.

Sebastian pointed at me and said, 'Bad fox.'

'He's a cute little fellow,' Bob said, and laughed when Sebastian sunk his teeth in my hand and said, 'Bad fox, bad fox, bad fox.'

No one so much as scolded him. Star is right. It's unbelievable what boys get away with.

Clems' father said, 'Clemmie was most upset she was unable to attend, but we were skiing.'

'Star sent me photos, though,' Clemmie piped up as she ran her Mason Pearson through her long straight blonde hair, which now hung below her waist.

'Yes, we, erm, thought the cake looked very lovely,' her parents agreed uncomfortably. Obviously they'd seen the tongue swallowing shot as txted by Star.

'Swell,' said Bob. Yes, he actually said 'swell.'

'You two make such a cute couple,' Indie told my parents.

Why does everyone keep saying my 'rents are cute? If I said 'swell,' the whole of England would take the piss for the next ten zillion years. Yet for some reason everything Bob and Sarah say or do is met with cries of, 'They're soooo cute.'

Hello Kitty toasters that toast Hello Kitty faces onto your bread are cute. Bob and Sarah are vaudevillian paragons if anything. Why can't they keep a pleasing balloon's distance between them at all times, like normal parents?

'Let's take Dorothy down to the pet shed,' I suggested to Clemmie, who had already taken my rabbit out of her carrier for a hop.

'Good idea,' she agreed as Dorothy gave her a punishing nip. Dorothy became quite the prima donna when left in her carrier for too long.

'I'll join you,' Indie added, checking her modelesque figure in the mirror as she rearranged her purple pash around her neck. 'Edwards, can you supervise the rest of the decorations?' she asked her valet. He gave her a little bow.

'We're going to take Dorothy down to the pet shed,' I told the loony madre and padre. They were still busy extolling the revolutionary effects of their remarriage to Clems' parents. Would you believe my father was talking about writing a script based on their rapprochement? That's what he was going to call his screenplay, *The Rapprochement*!

'Okay, bye, Calypso. Call us tomorrow and let us know how you're settling in,' Bob told me as he planted a kiss on my head.

Sarah, barely able to pull herself away from the conversation, just gave me the American hand sign for okay, which made my friends tear up with laughter. When I first pitched up in this land of rain and drizzle, I soon learned that it is not de rigueur to make hand gestures to people who are actually close enough to hear you speak. I suppose I should be glad she didn't try and high-five me. She does that too.

Sure enough, all the way down to the pet shed, Clemmie and Indie started dementedly hand-signing to one another. This is what the English do; take the piss (or as we say at school, extract the urine). It's a national pastime. Even the nuns and staff do it.

SEVEN

Operation Dumping Boys

Star was already standing in the snow-frosted pet run with her pet rat and snake. She was wearing her regulation Doc Martens (pink today), tartan mini-skirt and a ripped designer cashmere jumper. Her reticulated python, Brian, was slung around her neck like a pash, while Hilda the rat was peeping out her jumper, completing her rock royalty look. Even with punk accoutrements, Star still looked like a naughty cherub with her long strawberry-blonde hair, big green eyes and milky white skin.

I spotted Honey and Georgina sharing a fag in the trees of Pullers' Wood. From a distance they looked like sisters with their willowy figures and long blonde hair. Like Honey, Georgina's legs were completely exposed, but at least Georgina was wearing a black cashmere jumper and a baby blue pash around her neck as a nod to the weather. She was also hugging her teddy bear, Tobias, who is a full fee–paying student at Saint Augustine's.

After an excited session of air-kissing, Star pointed into the trees and smirked. 'Have you seen Honey's new bodyguard?'

I spotted the orange-robed Buddhist lurking in the woods nearby, seemingly in some deep meditation-type activity.

'Yaah, I saw him earlier. What's that about?' I asked.

'Honey's afraid there may be a plot to kidnap her now that her latest stepfather is in the House of Lords.'

'But, erm, aren't Buddhists meant to be all meditative and peaceful?' I asked.

'Yaah totally. But nonviolent security is really big at the moment. *Tatler* did some big spread on nonviolent security firms in Knightsbridge,' Clems explained.

I felt like fainting with the madness of it all, but then Georgina spotted us and came running over.

After another air-kiss-a-thon, I passed Dorothy to Georgina, who co-owns her with me. 'Dorothy! You've turned into a chubba lub!' she told our plump little rabbit through chattering teeth. 'You'll never be model-spotted now, darling.' She kissed Dorothy on the nose.

'Blame Sarah,' I told her, giving Dorothy's ears a little scratch. 'She wouldn't stop feeding her scraps even though I kept telling her, she's a sentient being and not a recycling bin!'

'Hilda's put on weight too,' Star said, referring to her pet rat. 'I've had to put her on the GI diet for rats. Mummy had a specialist flown out from New York to council her.'

The rest of us nodded gravely, as if having dietary specialists flown in to keep a rat's figure trim was a perfectly reasonable thing to do. When I first arrived at Saint Augustine's, I found everything about these spoilt, confident, sophisticated girls peculiar. I guess after you've lived with people long enough, though, you get used to their odd little ways.

When I was certain Honey couldn't hear us, I asked Georgina, 'Who's Honey rooming with?'

'Fenella and Perdita at Polo Central,' replied Georgina, referring to the polo twins.

Fenella and Perdita were not only identical twins but mad keen polo players. Their ponies were stabled nearby, and they were wildly popular with the polo boys at Eades who only spoke in polo-speak.

'It is seriously funny,' Georgina continued. 'Honey came to find me for a whinge. Apparently, every spare inch of wall space was already plastered with pictures of polo ponies and fit players by the time she arrived. She was absolutely livid, and Siddhartha, her security guard, kept telling her to breathe. Tobias laughed so hard he practically fell apart at the seams.'

We all knew how Tobias felt, because the first thing Honey did once her manservant had unpacked was to cover her pin board and wall space with paparazzi shots of herself. Honey adores society shots of herself chatting to other society clones. I could well imagine that she may have met her It Girl match with Fen and Perdita, who didn't rate anything outside the world of polo. They'd have absolutely no patience with Honey's bitchy humour, which meant Honey would have to hang out in someone else's room in order to get her bitch fix.

Oh no! Honey Hell, here I come.

Don't be so paranoid, I told myself. Honey would probably go to Georgina's room. After all, they went to nursery school together, and their bio fathers hunt together. 'What about you, Georgina, who are you rooming with?' I inquired idly, hoping it would be someone Honey-friendly.

'Beatrice and Izzie,' Georgina replied, failing to suppress her laughter. Izzie was quite scary, only in a less confrontational way than Honey.

I had heard on the txt-vine that Honey had pulled Izzie's boyfriend at some New Year's party in Val d'Isere. 'Is it true that Honey had a lip-fest with Izzie's boyfriend?' I asked now as my panic began to set in.

Star and Georgina looked at one another and burst out laughing. 'It was hilarious. When Izzie walked in and saw Honey in our room, she spat the dummy, darling. She gave Honey the most ferocious look, it almost melted Honey's collagen!'

'What did Honey do?' Clemmie asked, her Tiffany-box blue eyes wide with curiosity.

Georgina shrugged. 'You know Honey, she would have got on her high horse, but Izzie looked like she might slap her, so she brazened it out and denied everything. Put it this way; I don't think Honey will be visiting my room very much this term.'

I wasn't being paranoid. 'So hang on. If her room's out because of Fen and Perdita, and your room's out because of Izzie, where will Honey hang out?' I asked, trying to keep the desperation out of my voice.

'I'm rooming with Portia and Arabella,' Star said. 'So she won't *dare* come near us.'

'Don't worry, darling,' Indie said, reading my mind and throwing a comforting arm around me. 'She hates me too.'

This was true, but while Indie would give as good as she got where Honey was concerned, her presence alone might not be enough to keep Honey away. The fly in the ointment was Clemmie, who was soooo nice to everyone, including Honey. I had been Honey's torture toy from the day I arrived at Saint Augustine's. With my American accent, lack of grand ancestors or old money, I was a red flag to a mad bull. It was as inevitable as brown slops on a Sunday. Our room would become Honey's new torture parlour.

As if summoned by satanic forces, Honey tottered over to join us. Her orange-robed bodyguard followed at a serene distance. 'Laters, peasants. I'm going back up to the institution,' she groaned, flicking her butt at my feet as she sprayed herself with Febreze to get rid of the smoke smell. Then, confirming my worst fears, she added to Clemmie, 'I'll see you à la mo, Clems. I'll be hanging out in your room this term. Fen and Perdita are too polo for words, and I've soooo much to tell you, darling.'

'Laters,' Clemmie said, smiling sweetly at Honey.

'Laters,' we all added to Honey's blue-with-cold back. But for me, the word 'laters' held more than a touch of menace.

'I know she'll haunt our room,' I blurted after her entourage was out of earshot.

'So did you dump Freds?' Star asked, changing the subject in her usual radical way.

'Why on earth would I dump Freds?'

'Erm . . . because he makes you fall asleep and snore?'

'He soooo does not.'

'Well, he finds you disappointing.'

'Don't be mad. He does not find me disappointing.'

'Well, why did you say he did?'

'I didn't.'

'Yes, you did. And that's another thing. All you do is go on and on *ad infinitum* about Freds.'

I briefly toyed with the idea of fainting to avoid this tedious conversational cul-de-sac, but then Georgina agreed with Star. 'We *do* spend far too much time obsessing over boys.'

I looked from girl to girl. I was suddenly surrounded by an anti-boy cult. 'Boys are a vital part of existence!' I reminded them.

'I quite like boys. Well, pulling boys anyway,' Clemmie added. She was looking practically as horrified as me.

Indie didn't look too keen on the boy-dumping idea either. She hadn't said anything, but I was almost certain-ish she'd been fantasising about Malcolm all through the holidays.

Star looked directly at her as she said, 'I'm going to be more like Indie and focus on my music.'

Indie nodded expressionlessly, blinded by the brightness of Star's million-watt personality. There was also the small detail that Indie hadn't actually pulled Malcolm yet.

'What about Malcolm?' I tested Indie.

'Who's Malcolm?' she asked, blinking her chocolaty eyes with confusion – as if she wasn't sick with love for him at all.

I looked around at my friends. They were all in this Dumping Freddie scheme together. It was a cabal of evil.

So I fainted.

EIGHT

In Defence of the Realm

'I'm not dumping Freds,' I told Star firmly after she'd put Brian on top of me to bring me round. She had even made him give me a little kiss with his flicky-out tongue. 'It's taken me all my life to pull a prince and I'm not about to throw him back now, just as things are going well.' I passed Brian back.

'We can still pull boys, though, can't we?' pleaded Clemmie again. Pulling boys was, after all, her favourite sport. The thing about Clemmie was, once she'd pulled them, she tossed them right back. And she never thought about them again.

Star ignored her. Placing her hands on my shoulders, she looked straight into my eyes. 'You'll be too busy for Freds, darling. Apart from your fencing and your GCSEs, you promised to help Indie and me with our lyrics, remember.'

Whoops. I had almost forgotten about agreeing to write lyrics for Star and Indie's band. Their main interest was writing miserable minor chord compositions about the horrors of being rock royalty – or in Indie's case, real royalty – and going to the most exclusive boarding school in England. Love them though I do, their songs made me feel like attending my own funeral. Star knows that lyrics aren't her strong point, so when Indie came to the school with her guitar last term, Star started harbouring a dream that the three of us would combine our talents for the greater good of music. She'd sing and play bass, Indie would play lead guitar – or 'the six strings of the devil,' as Father Conway calls it – and I'd write the words.

'But I haven't written anything yet,' I admitted. 'I mean, with Bob and Sarah here and –'

'I know, that's exactly what I'm talking about. We've all got soooo much going on. Boys will just be in the way. Besides, Freds is too freakishly normal for you.'

I wished she'd stop saying that.

'Star's right,' Georgina said as she placed Dorothy on the snow-frosted grass for a hop.

'Et tu, Georgina?' I cried, shoving an imagined dagger into my heart.

She nudged me affectionately. 'Pulling boys is fun, but the whole boyfriend saga has become très, très, très boring, darling. No offence, Calypso.'

'But what about love?' I asked, deeply offended.

'Now *I* feel like fainting,' Star groaned. 'I dumped Kev, and he was low maintenance, darling.' What she really meant was, he did anything she said. 'Freddie is *far* too high maintenance.'

'He's not a GI diet,' I said crossly. 'He's my boyfriend.

Whatever happened to "for better or worse"? It's not as if we're together twenty-four-seven or anything sad like that. I'm here at school all the time. Well, apart from exeats and weekends after Saturday classes.'

'How many times a day do you txt him?' Georgina asked me as she plaited her long, blonde, obedient hair.

'I don't know. A few.' I shrugged, running a hand through my own rebellious blonde locks that never obeyed a single command.

'Over twenty?' Star asked, folding her arms and contorting her gorgeous features, taking on the expression of a menopausal matron.

I shrugged again. 'Maybe. I don't exactly chalk them up.' I tried to flick my hair in a careless gesture of defiance, but it got stuck to my lip-gloss and I spent the next few minutes wiping it off. I picked up Dorothy, partly because I thought her little paws might be frozen but mostly for emotional comfort. She was all wiggly and eager to be put back down.

'Okay, so, let's say you txt him twenty times a day,' Georgina suggested. 'Then, for argument's sake, let's say he txts you back twenty times. That's forty txts you're reading and rereading.'

'You're scarily good at hard sums, darling,' I told her sarcastically. Then to be horrible, I teased, 'Maybe you should marry Mr Templeton?' Mr Templeton was our horrible little maths teacher who would have put even dear old Einstein off his hard sums.

But all Georgina did was roll her eyes.

'Plus, you agonise for ages and ages over your txts. And then you analyse whatever he txts you,' Star added.

'That is soooo untrue,' I lied.

Star and the others all giggled. I suppose I have forwarded a lot of my txts to Star before sending them to Freds. But still, she shouldn't have put the Doc Marten in like that.

'I've had soooo many conversations with you, Calypso, agonising over the number of kisses you should send Freddie and analysing the significance of how many he sends to you. And then there are all those txts you forward me.'

Talk about betrayal. 'Hah!' was all I could say to my traitor of a friend. I looked to Clemmie and Indie for support, but their eyes remained fixed on Star. Star can be très, très persuasive.

'I just think we should get the whole boy thing into perspective, Calypso.'

'What does "into perspective" mean?' I asked, rolling my eyes like a loon.

'Spending less time focusing on boyfriends and more time focusing on the things we really want to do, like music and writing.'

'I just like pulling boys, really,' Clemmie piped up.

I loved Clemmie.

Star looked at our boy-mad friend and smiled. 'Pulling them is fine, I'm not talking about that. It's just once you start hanging out too much with one boy and daydreaming about him, it becomes a pain.'

I didn't find daydreaming about Freds the least bit painful. But I didn't say anything. He was the perfect boyfriend. He had the most lovely sticky-outy black hair and kissable lips and he always made me feel wonderful, apart from when he gave me disappointed looks. But that hadn't happened for, well, since the other day. Which proved he must be getting used to my odd ways. Which meant now was not the time to dump him.

Star clicked her fingers in front of my face. 'See! Look at yourself, Calypso. You're drifting off into Freddieland right now. I can see it in your eyes. They've gone all moon-shaped.'

And so another circus of laughter ensued.

A snowflake landed on my nose. As more flakes followed, I put my hands out to catch them. I usually loved it when it snows, but all I felt then was a horrible sense of doom. My mother calls me the Queen of Doomsday Prophesies. But then again she also thinks boys will respect me more if I wear Wellies.

'How did Kev take the dump?' I asked Star, hoping to divert attention away from Freds and me.

'Oh, he cried,' Star replied. If it wasn't Star, I would have sworn I detected a wobble in her voice. 'And then I cried,' she added. 'It was quite the cry-fest, actually.'

'That's really sad,' I told her, but all she did was shrug as we both watched the white snowflakes falling on her pink Doc Martens.

'Yaah, but then I told myself: Indie, Calypso and I are

going to be flat out with Sloaney Trash, and I did a cartwheel.'

'What's Sloaney Trash?' asked Clemmie.

'That's what we're calling the band,' Indie told her. 'We only decided last night.'

'Nice of you to tell *me*.' I sulked.

'We did phone,' Indie said. 'And we can still change it. It's just an idea, but we thought you'd like the ironic angle.'

'We didn't just call once either,' Star added. 'We called and called and called. Your mobile was engaged.'

Whoops-a-daisy. I was on the phone with Freds all night. They'd only left one voice mail and by the time I got it, it was really late.

'I'm tucking Dorothy up in the pet shed before she freezes,' Georgina said as she dashed off.

'Indie's got some fab ideas for lyrics,' Star said as she scraped her foot through the thin veil of snow. 'The music wing's finished now and we've got the use of the studio. You've always wanted to be a proper writer. Aren't you excited, Calypso?'

'Yaah, of course,' I replied hesitantly.

I should have known better. Star was always trying to push me towards my dreams. Last term, she had persuaded me to enter a national newspaper's essay competition. The winner hadn't been announced yet. Not that I would win or anything. At least I hoped not. The rules were to give an autobiographical account of suffering or trauma in a teen-ager's life. I'd opted to write about the pain of my own parents' madder-than-mad, short-lived split, only I had to use a little artistic licence to spice it up.

I know it was *meant* to be autobiographical, but who wants to read about a boring old couple having a midlife crisis? No one, that's who. And anyway, how was I to know that no sooner had I handed it in, than they'd go and reunite like love's young dream? I would die a thousand deaths if I did actually win, because then it would be published in the national press, and Bob and Sarah would read it and kill me.

Star nudged me. 'Are you okay, Calypso?' she asked.

'Yaah, I was just thinking about the essay. They're judging it soon.'

'Oh my God,' she squealed, clamping her hand over her mouth.

'Imagine if you win?' Clemmie said.

Then Star said something truly horrifying 'Think of it, the whole country reading your essay.'

'Sarah and Bob are back together now and totally in love. They'd die if they read what I wrote – after they kill me first,' I said.

'I'm sure you're just being paranoid,' Star insisted, trying to wrap Brian around my neck again. It is a major strugglerama, trying to pretend I like Brian all the time. 'You worry too much, darling. You overanalyse everything.'

'I do not!' I protested, even though it was true.

'You always have. And since you've added a boy like Freds to your list of things to fret about, you've turned into a lovesick puppy who can't think of anything but him.' Star grabbed me by the shoulders again and looked into my eyes as if about to hypnotise me. 'You're fifteen, Calypso. Life's just beginning. You need to live a little! I mean, it's not as if you're going to marry him, is it?'

Isn't it? Okay, so it probably isn't, but I still couldn't believe she was saying all this. Well, I could. She's never been a Freddie fan, but more worrisome than that, she was also stubborn, and in all the time I'd known her, I'd never known her to let something drop. Take the essay thing. There was no way I would have written that essay if Star hadn't made me.

'Come on, my legs are blue,' Georgina urged, having returned from putting Dorothy in the luxurious heated pet shed. 'Quick, peasants, let's leg it before we turn to snow statues.'

Back at the dorm, all had been transformed. The 'rents had gone home, and Indie's people had turned our bedroom into an interior design magazine spread. There were purple velvet cushions embroidered with gold crests strewn across the room, and our beds were draped in purple velvet splendour. The old oil paintings of saints and the bright red panic buttons by the beds were all that remained to remind us we were at school. The panic buttons had been installed recently, and as far as I knew, they'd never been used. But as I flopped on my bed, I had an overwhelming urge to press mine.

NINE

Enterprising Initiatives

We were all sprawled on our beds, listening to our iPods, scrolling through txt messages and listlessly flicking through magazines, when Miss Bibsmore hobbled into our room. She'd gone back to wrapping carpet and duct tape around her walking stick, so we hadn't heard her approach.

"Ello, girls,' she screeched.

I think I speak for all when I say her appearance came as a shock. I mean, Miss Bibsmore's no runway model at the best of times, but that evening she was crumpled over her stick even farther than usual. More freakish than that, she was wearing a massive pair of fluffy dog slippers with big floppy ears and plastic stick-on eyes. Animal slippers are de rigueur for house spinsters, so it was really the tatty old dressing gown over the floral flannel nightie that cracked me up.

'Are you alright, Miss Bibsmore?' I asked, slightly concerned by her appearance.

'Don't you worry about me, luvvie. I'm just feeling a bit

orf – it's the menopause, you see. My womb hurts something chronic and my back's playing up. It's a cruel god that cursed us with these 'ormones, dearie, I'll tell you that for free,' she said.

As if anyone would pay for that gem of philosophy! None of us really knew how to respond, so we just nodded.

'All unpacked I see,' Miss Bibsmore remarked with approval. 'Not like some I could mention.' She was looking at the door as she spoke, and I turned to see Honey.

'What will you be after then, Madam?' Miss Bibsmore asked my anti-friend. 'This isn't your room last time I looked.'

Honey's always doing battle with house spinsters, or anyone else she sees as inferior, which is basically anyone who doesn't want to take her photograph and place it in *Tatler*. The exception was Miss Bibsmore, who wasn't in the least bit rattled by Honey's poisonous put-downs. Which was probably why all Honey said was, 'Oh, shut up, you insane old woman,' before walking off in a huff. Mild by Honey's standards.

'How was your Christmas, Miss Bibsmore?' Indie, Clemmie and I asked as we each took one of our two earphones out.

'Oh, it was triffic, luvvies, simply triffic.' Her eyes travelled about the room, which was clean, thankfully. 'Lovely job you've done on the room, girls,' she remarked, hobbling across the room to feel the fabric of the curtains. 'That'd be silk an' all. Real class, that's what that is and it'll be all your work, I'll hazard, Your Highness,' she said to Indie.

'I really wish you'd call me Indie, Miss Bibsmore,' Indie told her, while continuing to rock her head in time to the music.

'Oh, I couldn't do that, Your Highness,' Miss Bibsmore said, horrified by the thought. 'It wouldn't be right, not with you being proper royal an' all,' she insisted.

The truth was, there were a number of royals at my school, including a few princesses, loads of countesses and ladies and the odd duchess. But none of them got royal highness-ed like Indie. Using your title at school was considered *de trop*. Freds is next in line to the throne but even he never uses his title. The plain truth was, Indie had charmed her way into Miss Bibsmore's heart.

'Well I'll be off then. Me rheumatism is playing up something rotten,' she moaned. 'Mind you, don't get muck on the princess's spreads with those shoes of yours, Miss Fraser Marks,' she warned Clemmie.

'Deffo,' replied Clemmie, scrutinising her *Tatler*.

'And 'ow's your poor mother, Miss Kelly? Staying on a bit in England by all reports now yer father is up and joined 'er.'

'Yes, Miss Bibsmore.'

'That must be nice for you, luvvie. I 'eard as much. It's the nuns, yer see. They like a good natter. Not that I'm one for gossip nor nothing.'

'No, Miss Bibsmore,' we all agreed in the Saint Augustine's tone of perceived obedience and respect.

'Well, I'll be gittin back on my rounds, then. Cheerio, girls. Good-bye, Your Highness.'

'Bye, Miss Bibsmore,' we called after her, as if her visit had been the highlight of our day.

'What do you think of Star's idea about our dumping our boyfriends?' I asked casually, as if I wasn't at all desperate for support from my roommates.

'I don't have a boyfriend,' Indie replied as she lazily scrolled through her txts on her little bejewelled purple phone.

'What about Malcolm?' I asked, hoping to rattle her.

Indie was saved from responding by Clemmie, who blurted, 'She didn't say we couldn't *pull* boys, just that we shouldn't get all clingy about any one boy in particular.'

I looked over at Indie, but she was still scrolling away, seemingly unbothered by Star's Operation Dumping Boys.

I decided to visit Lady Portia Herrington Briggs. She was on the national sabre team with me and had been my fencing partner since Star had chucked sabre to focus on her minor chord compositions. Given that Star and Portia were sharing this term, I wondered if Star would start giving Portia grief about her boyfriend, who happened to be Kev's older brother, Billy. The dating habits of English public schools are très, très incestuous.

Portia is blessed with one of those cool aristocratic demeanours. She's aloof without being in the least bit arrogant. I've never seen her ruffled or rattled or acting loopy like other teenagers. Even when we fence, her luxuriously thick, long raven mane remains hair-commercial perfect. If she wasn't so lovely and sweet, her perfection could easily mark her out for secret hatred. As it is, no one has a bad word to say about her, not that she's a pushover. Even Honey tempers her psycho-toff rants when Portia's around.

When I walked in, Star, Portia and Arabella had a Lower Sixth girl in their room selling ghastly handmade jewelry as part of the school's Enterprise Awareness scheme. The scheme claimed to provide girls with the skills needed to be entrepreneurial businesswomen. I think that was stretching it. The fact of the matter was the students only bought whatever the Lower Sixth came up with because the proceeds went towards the Sunday Supper, which was a treat our year was now privileged to enjoy.

I picked up one of the gaudy plastic beads on coloured string and asked how much it was.

'A tenner. We're doing a really cool music night and getting in the caterers from Eades to do a proper Burns Night feast,' the older girl explained. 'Sans haggis, naturally.'

'What will you pipe in then?' I asked, relieved as I relived the memory of last year's horrible haggis. Burns Night is one of those mad Scottish traditions like caber tossing, reeling and kilt wearing. The Scots really are exquisitely bonkers. Take Clems and Malcolm for example. Burns Night is a cool idea though as it's the celebration of their national poet – and there isn't enough celebrating of national poets, if you ask me.

'A giant pizza,' the Sixth girl replied.

'Cool.'

'The real news is that we're performing,' Star added, holding out an arm covered in coloured bead bracelets. 'So buy up big darling.' Even though most of the Enterprise Initiative products are often revolting bits of jewelry or hoodies with mad slogans emblazoned across them, we all buy and wear them. It's sort of a cult thing. Occasionally they even turn up on eBay, where they are snatched up for exorbitant sums of money by girls who missed out. The trouble is that these cult items bring new depth to the saying "so last term." No girl would be seen dead in last term's Enterprise Initiative.

'Wow, that's really cool about you and Indie playing. Does Indie know?' I asked.

'No, but I've told you,' Star insisted, 'because I want you to write something for it. It will be our first big gig, and if it goes well, we can lay down the tracks on CD,' she explained. 'You did say you wanted to write some songs for us.' Her green eyes were sparkling with infectious enthusiasm, and in that moment I decided she was probably right. Not about the boy thing, but about focusing on our dreams. It wouldn't do me any harm to try my hand at writing lyrics.

'I'm on the case,' I assured her as I studied the bracelet horrors I was about to blow my term allowance on. 'I'm just waiting for the, erm . . . inspiration.'

Star rolled her eyes and shook her head at my dismal lie. The best and worst thing about best friends is they know you so well.

I purchased a bundle of plastic bead horrors, and when groups of girls started piling into the room, I snuck off down to the pet shed and rang Freddie.

'Hey,' he answered. 'What's up?'

'Just wanted to hear your voice,' I told him as I watched Hilda running herself ragged on her little rat wheel. 'And to make sure we're still on for Saturday afternoon,' I added casually, in case, like Star, he thought I was a lovesick puppy.

'Definitely,' he agreed, before ruining my life by adding, 'unless something comes up.'

TEN

Peace, Love and Buddhist Security

The next day, Clemmie, Indie and I slept through the 6:45 a.m. bell. Miss Bibsmore had to come and poke us in the ribs with her stick after the third bell. By then it was 7:10, giving us twenty minutes to clean our teeth, get dressed into our vile uniforms and leg it to the ref and devour what food we could before chapel. I couldn't find any of my horrible maroon pleated skirts.

Clems offered me one of hers, which was indecently short on me. I'd definitely get a blue if not an ASBO for lewdity.

Fortunately, after four years, we were all experts in the art of flying down the narrow stone steps. In the ref, we grabbed a couple of croissants (one for each pocket) and gulped a hot chocolate each.

Mass had already started by the time we crept into the chapel. Father Conway was banging on about how our mortal bodies belong to Our Lady and that we shouldn't allow anyone to defile them. I hoped the nurse from the infirmary was listening. She was always defiling our bodies with violent needle jabs.

As if reading my mind, Indie whispered, 'We'd best remind Sister in the infirmary about that next time she gives us our flu jabs,' which sent me off giggling.

We always had a full Latin mass on the first day back. After that it was just a twenty-minute prayer and hymn service, unless it was a feast day. I heard my tummy rumbling and was madly tempted to sneak-eat my pocket croissants, but not even Honey would be that sacrilegious. Eventually Father Conway wrapped up his sermon with a fervent wish that this would be another successful academic term, and being a new year, an *annus mirabilis*.

After mass we had to race back upstairs for room inspection. I had another look for my buggery skirts, but they had obviously done a runner. Probably too embarrassed to be seen on my freakishly long stick-like legs.

I was so self-conscious of how high Clem's skirt was riding up that I developed a special bent-knee run, pulling the skirt down as I scuttled about the corridors, which was how I happened to bump into Honey's new security guy. I'd like to see the kidnapper brave enough to take on Honey. Not that this man in orange robes looked particularly hard. Maybe he would meditate the kidnappers into surrender?

'Sorry, miss,' he said as my head hit his orange-robed knees.

Sister Constance wasn't too keen on personal security guards. At Eades they were part of the furniture. They even had their own housing block, which had resulted in all sorts of tragic nobodies hiring security just to show off.

'That's okay,' I told him. 'It was totally my fault.' Then I waddled off, still tugging my skirt down while Honey screamed about how she would sue the knickers off me if I damaged her bodyguard.

'What's wrong?' Portia asked after she'd watched me waddle into class and take my seat beside her in Latin. Only four of us were doing Latin for our GCSEs. For some unfathomable reason, parents find small classes a good thing. But then they're not the ones having to defend themselves against the madness of Miss Mills and her ilk without backup.

'My skirts have done a runner,' I explained. 'Clems leant me one of hers, but it's too short.

Portia smiled. 'You can borrow mine, darling. At least we're closer in height. Listen, I didn't get to finish the translations we were meant to do over the break. Do you think Miss Mills will believe me if I say, *Canis meus id comedit?*'

I laughed, remembering the translations we'd amused ourselves with during dull Latin lectures last term. 'Your dog ate it?'

'Too obvious, you think?'

'Here,' I said, passing my book over. 'You'd better copy mine.' Some loopy Lower Sixth girls had told me that dead languages were easy A grades. 1 thought that meant I could snooze and gossip my way through class, but Miss Mills ruined that little illusion quick smart. As she entered the room that morning, she rambled off the old *In nomine patras, et filie et spirtitus sancti*, then started gabbing away *ad absurdum* about how much work we were expected to put in this term.

What did she think Latin was, exactly? A living language? Honestly, teachers are a breed apart. This was proved beyond doubt when she passed us a booklet titled – and I'm not making this up – *How to Pass Your Exams (And Enjoy Yourself)*.

Honestly, I don't know why I bother attending classes at all sometimes. The picture on the front of the booklet depicted a skateboarder. Now what, I ask you, has skateboarding got to do with passing your Latin GCSE? Nothing, that's what. For a start, skateboards and the clothes that go with them are banned at our school.

Things didn't get better when Miss Mills urged us to open our booklet, where saying after pithy saying urged us to do unnatural things like, 'Convert linear notes to MIND MAPS.'

I turned to a page decorated in wizards, fat television show hosts and musical scores urging us to learn, 'VISUALLY, ORALLY, AURALLY and KINAESTHETICALLY.' Portia and I looked at each other and shook our heads.

I passed Portia a note.
I just bumped into Honey's security guy in the corridor.
She passed one back.
He seems weirdly nice for a Honey person?
I wrote back:
Who'd want to steal Honey, though?

Portia wrote:

Maybe someone out there's got a hit on her?

I responded:

No one asked me to chip in.

And then we started laughing like that Laughing Cavalier chap that hangs in the Wallace Collection in London. We went there on an art excursion in Year Eight although Star and I nicked off to Selfridges and tried on wigs. It was still très, très culturally enhancing, I assure you.

We were laughing so feverishly that I actually fell off my chair. Even Portia, with her aloof demeanour and centuries of breeding, only barely managed to keep her balance.

Miss Mills loomed over me as I lay sprawled on the floor. But instead of saying something charitable and nice like 'Are you all right, dear?' she snatched up our notes and read them.

I'm sure that reading the personal correspondence of other people can't be legal. Still, I thought hopefully, even horrible old Miss Mills must see the joke? But no, instead of joining in our circus of hilarity, she made us stay back and translate our notes into Latin after class. Honestly, some teachers really should be sectioned under the Lack of Humour Act.

Her stupid punishment made us late for our lunchtime fencing practice. We ran like mad things down the corridors. Well, I ran like a mad thing because I had to do a sort of running waddle so I could keep my knickers covered with Clem's tiny skirt. As we took a short pause while passing a nun, I asked Portia about Billy, hoping to garner support against Star's Dumping Boys crusade.

'I've dumped him,' she said.

I fainted.

Okay, I didn't actually faint, because then Portia nudged me and said, 'Just joking, darling.'

But then she added, 'We *are* on a break, though. At least until after the GCSEs. We agreed it would be too stressful, especially now we're both on the national team. I'm really excited about going to Italy, aren't you, darling? I hear the Italian fencing standard is the best in the world after the Hungarians. Basically Billy and I agreed to prioritise fencing and exams.'

Then I actually did faint.

Honey's Buddhist guard helped me up – and saw my knickers, which was mortifying because they were a pair that had once been white but had turned grey in the wash.

Honey had a total Honey Fit. 'What the bloody hell do you think you're doing using my security? And as for you, Siddhartha, you are supposed to have your eyes on your principle at all times. Someone could have kidnapped *me* while you were touching her.'

Siddhartha looked ashamed. 'Sorry, Miss,' he said to his principle.

'My father's paying you to guard *me*, not *her*,' she shrieked, pointing one of her long talons at me. 'Why would anybody want to steal *her*?'

ELEVEN

Not Fair Was Made to Fare

Portia and I had to run off because we were having another laughing fit and didn't want to get a stitch before fencing. Now that we had been selected for the national team and were heading off to Italy for our first international tournament, we had pledged to devote as much time as we could to extra practice. The Italian fencing team was one of the best in the world, which was a bit daunting.

Our South African fencing master, Bell End, was as mad as a drawer of old ladies' knickers. He was sitting on the floor, reading *Sword* magazine. He didn't look up when we came in so we sailed past him, through the armoury and into the changing rooms. We were both feverish with excitement, as this would be the first time we would be fencing with our GBR international kit.

The outfits fit so perfectly, we did some Milanese modelling struts and said 'Mama mia' and 'Ooh la la.'

It was one of those blissfully va-va-va-voom moments that I will never forget. Actually, I could quite fancy myself in my new gear. I couldn't wait to show it off to Freds. It was all so feverishly exciting.

When we came out, Bell End was still on the floor reading his magazine, only now he was lying facedown, his head propped on his hands. I looked at Portia and she looked at me in that way you do when wondering if a teacher has reached the straightjacket stage.

I did my 'this is awkward' cough.

Portia slapped me on the back and asked, 'Is this an inconvenient time, sir?' with all the serenity you'd expect of true nobility.

Bell End looked up at us as if we were strangers. 'I'm not in the mood for fencing,' he replied gruffly.

'Shall we come back later perhaps, Mr Wellend?' she inquired, remembering to use his real name.

'If you like,' he muttered like a sullen child.

Talk about exasperating. 'But sir, we've got our first international tournament in Italy to prepare for,' I protested, ignoring Portia's warning look. Honestly, if I had had a Bibsmore stick, I would have poked him with it.

Bell End looked up at me and smiled. 'There's the spirit, Kelly! Don't take no for an answer.' Then he jumped up with the agility you expect from an Olympic Silver medal winner and slapped me on the back so hard I'm pretty certain he dislodged a few vital organs. For a short little stout South African, he's fiercely muscular.

'Right! Let's be having you first, Kelly. Briggsie, wire her up.'

Portia wired me up.

Bell End grabbed a sabre and mask from the salle d'armes and wired himself to the electrical device that would record our points. He saluted me with his embarrassing signature salute. Oh my God, it was soooo tragic. His blade made a threatening swishing sound as he carved the letter *W* in the air.

He called 'play' and began an aggressive shuffle towards me using the funny little steps you spend most of your fencing career practicing.

'I'm Italian, an arrogant, unpredictable nasty bit of work,' he told me in his thick South African accent as he made a swiping lunge.

What was it with teachers and role-playing? Was there something in their curriculum that recommended it? If so, the suits who come up with these things should be lined up against a wall and pelted with water balloons, I thought, only to realise too late that Bell End had pulled back his sabre and punched the blade into my chest.

'Ow, that hurt,' I gasped over the buzz of the electrical point recorder.

You're not really meant to hit your opponent overly hard, but Bell End knew, as I did, that while you could be carded for overly aggressive play, you could usually get away with a lot before that red card came your way.

Bell End chuckled mercilessly at my agony as I limped back to the *en guard* line clutching my ribs.

Teachers are soooo hilarious.

He called 'play' again.

We advanced down the piste. I was sore but determined to avenge myself. Bell End was still pressing on with his role-play. 'Yes, my father's father was killed in a duel. I myself am prepared to play dirty.' Seriously, his fake Italian accent was a shocker.

The man was a clinical case study in lunacy. I'm sure the school could make a fortune selling his mind to science and build all the new science wings they want, I was thinking as Bell End gained priority once again and stole the point. All these intellectual musings on the fencing piste were costing me dearly. I know it will be a huge loss to the world, but I think I shall have to abandon philosophy as a calling if I plan to distinguish myself as a sabreur.

'I am a molto-talented player,' my master taunted dementedly from the en garde line before calling 'play' again. 'I took my first baby step in the salle, and I know all the tricks,' he ranted away as we advanced towards one another purposefully. 'I know that for every red card I get, I'll still get away with a few illegal manoeuvres.' He laughed like a crazy man.

I lunged.

'I'm smart enough to stop short of eviction, though,' he warned as he deftly slipped his blade under mine and executed a cut to my arm, knocking my sabre clean out of my hand. And then, to add insult to injury, he thwacked me across the legs as I was grappling impotently with the sword dangling pathetically from its wires.

'That is soooo not legal!' I shouted through the plastic guard of my mask. 'The legs aren't even a target!'

'Quite right, Kelly.' He snickered. 'The naughty Italian girl will be issued with a warning, but not a red card yet, I hazard. She likes seeing her opponents unnerved,' Bell End said nastily. 'Are you unnerved, Kelly? Are you frightened? Is your belly filled with butterflies and your mind trembling with terror?'

'Yes, of course I'm bloody unnerved. My fencing master is the apex of loondom. What pupil in her right mind wouldn't be unnerved?' I yelled back at him.

He continued to play with a reckless disregard for the rules of engagement. Every time I pointed out a breech of rules or etiquette to him he'd either say, 'Ah, but the president didn't see that' or 'Quite right, Kelly. Another yellow card to the naughty Italian.'

When I realised the victory was about to be stolen from me by a cheating nutcase with schizophrenic disorders, it all got too much for me. After another illegal point was awarded to the 'nasty Italian girl,' I completely flipped.

I tore off my mask so I could fight my corner properly. Turning to my friend, I said, 'That point was illegal. Portia, you saw that!'

Portia went to open her mouth, but Bell End put his hand up before she could get a word out. 'That's a red card to you, Kelly, for removing your mask during play. Your opponent couldn't be happier. Your mistake has put her only one point away from victory. If this is how you intend to play in Italy in two weeks, you may as well buy yourself a clown suit now!'

'Daft fool,' I muttered as I angrily shoved my mask back on. I bet none of the other members of the national team had to suffer the indignity of a fencing master like Bell End. I bet they all had nice, reasonable, polished masters with poise and decorum and a sense of fair play.

But in the words of someone who had time for idle thoughts, 'ours is not to reason why, ours is but to do or die.' And to that end, if we were playing dirty I would play dirtier. The next point would be mine. I would make bloody sure of it. No nutty South African with a bad Italian accent was going to cheat me out of victory.

I executed a flawless lunge and hit Bell End slap bang in the middle of his chest. Hah!

I paused, the way you do awaiting for the victorious buzz of the recorder, but no pleasing sound came. Nothing. In my pause, Bell End cut his sabre down on mine, releasing a deafening buzz that declared the victory his.

I tore off my mask. My eyes were flashing with fury. 'But I hit *you*!' I insisted. 'Portia saw it. You must have felt it, sir!' I was furious now. There was no way I was conceding that point. No buggery way. 'There must be something wrong with your lamé!' I insisted, chucking my sabre down the piste.

'Well spotted, naive little American girl. You will do

well next time to be sure all electrics are working *before* the game has started instead of waiting until after your opponent's victory. If you call foul after the match like that in Italy, it will look tacky and mean-spirited, Kelly.'

I couldn't believe it. This was wrong for soooo many reasons. 'But I tested my sabre on your lamé before play and it was working!' I told him.

'Ah yes, so you did, Miss Kelly. So tell me, how did the naughty Italian girl cheat you of your victory?'

I wasn't going to be drawn. 'Fine,' I said churlishly. 'The naughty Italian won,' I agreed, turning to leave. I didn't think fainting would be an effective weapon in my fight against Bell End. He'd probably run me through with his sabre while I was lying in a helpless heap.

'Don't give in to defeat so easily, Kelly. Look here.'

'What?' I said, turning back to face him.

'This little switch here,' he said, removing his sabre from the electrical wire and pointing inside the guard. 'It allows me to switch my electrics on or off as suits me.' He passed his sabre over to me to examine.

'Oh, my giddy aunt!' I gasped as I saw the small switch concealed inside the guard. 'Check this out, Portia.'

Bell End looked delighted as we examined his tricked-out sabre. 'Didn't you watch the Olympic DVDs?' he asked.

I vaguely remembered an incident where a fencer was disqualified for having just such a switch inside his guard. 'But that guy was disqualified,' I said now.

'Only because they found him out, Kelly. The fool triggered the switch when his opponent was nowhere near the combat area. Your opponents in Italy may not be so stupid. The lesson for today, girls, is don't trust anyone.'

Bell End then went on to fence Portia in a completely clean and reasonable way. She totally rinsed him.

Life is soooo unfair. I probably would have gone into a deep sulk if Bell End hadn't handed us our tickets to Florence. 'Your first international tournament is in two weeks' time. Tickets and accommodations all courtesy of your sponsors. Make sure you distinguish yourselves, and maybe next time they'll send you business class. More to the point, I don't want my name dragged through the dirt by a couple of big girls' blouses.'

'No, Mr Wellend,' we replied, clutching our tickets to our chests and bouncing up and down.

I'd never been to Italy. 'I wonder how Italians kiss,' I mused as Portia and I were changing. 'Not that I intend on trying them out or anything, but one does wonder.'

'Does *one*?' Portia asked, raising one eyebrow in that special aristocratic way she has.

'I was born with a naturally inquisitive nature, Portia, that's all. Of course I'm completely happy with Freds, who happens to be the best kisser in the world. No Italian Lothario holds the slightest attraction for moi, darling.'

She slapped me across the legs with her smelly vest, and I slapped her with mine. Italy was going to be très, très cool with bells on!

TWELVE

Buddhist Security Alert

That night we had an illegal post-lights-out party in our room. After four years we were accomplished at post-lights-out parties, which Star thinks should be encouraged rather than banned.

I agree. I mean, they force us to do all sorts of other mad things, like three-legged-racing and javelin throwing. But if we were to go about chucking javelins and tearing through Windsor with our legs tied together, the school would have a lot to answer for. And anyway, what reasonable adult actually expects girls our age to go to bed before midnight? None, that's how many.

Indie pulled the bin away from the door so Miss Bibsmore couldn't hear our whispers. Then Honey lit up a fag and suggested we play one of her psycho-toff games called 'If you were a piece of fruit, what would you be?' 'For example, people would think of me as a star fruit because I'm exotic, expensive and sweet,' she explained, her implausibly long lashes flapping about her face like blinds.

'Shall we not play that game?' Portia sighed. She was knitting – or trying to knit – a scarf for her father. It was looking more like a swizzle stick, but I could tell she had big hopes for it, so I didn't say anything.

But Honey pressed on. 'And Calypso would probably be, say, an apple. Cheap and common. Now what would Star be?' she asked, struggling to wrinkle her Botox-bulging brow in thought.

'A fruit fly,' Star snapped, squirting Honey with Febreze. 'Blow your smoke out the window and let the rest of us talk about something *real* now, please?'

Honey waved the smoke away from her own face. Because she knows smoking causes wrinkles, she has developed this mad way of smoking where she holds her cigarette at arm's length, brings it in for a quick puff and extends her arm again. Then she blows the smoke in another direction, usually at my face. 'Fine, we can talk about what I got up to on my hols, darlings,' she conceded. 'I was soooo wildly popular in Val d'Isere this year. It must be my new breast implants. I had *every* designer begging me to wear their clothes at this season's shows. Every club owner was grovelling for me to make an *entrance* at their club. I had to keep telling them, "darlings, I'm just one gorgeous It Girl, and as generous as I am, I can't be everywhere at once, can I?"' Then she did her little honky toff laugh and went on with other tales of how she'd impressed, adored and papped.

It was like a psychotic bedtime story.

I began to nod off at the start of a story of how some alcohol brand had asked her to be their new face. 'They said they wanted something young, fresh and exotic.'

'So basically they could simply use a star fruit and save on costs?' Star asked faux-innocently.

I swear, if there had been a bomb in the room you could have heard it tick. The silence was broken by Georgina, who asked about my weekend with the royal family.

'Oh, my giddy aunt! I forgot to tell you, they don't even have cable.'

The whole room gasped.

'Tell her about the disappointed looks Freds kept giving you,' Star urged.

'Disappointed looks?' Georgina repeated, looking confused.

Star shook her head in disgust.

I glared at her, furious at her betrayal. 'Erm, well, Star's exaggerating really.'

Then Star started up about how Freds was a boring idiot unworthy of her best friend, so I interrupted with the story of how I'd faked a cold to avoid going on the shoot.

'Did you use the chili oil on—,' Georgina asked.

'It was a clay pigeon shoot,' Star explained, delving into the marshmallow bag on the floor.

'Well, I didn't know it was a clay pigeon shoot at the time, did I? I thought they were off to murder lovely living birds, like grouse or pheasants or something.'

Honey looked so shocked, I thought her face had

moved. 'Only chavs, foreigners and peasants of the lowest order shoot birds in January,' she spat at me. 'They're too fat and slow at this time of year. It's bad sportsmanship. Besides, it's not even grouse season.'

'Whatever! How was I meant to know when you shoot grouse? I'm not sure I've *seen* a grouse, and even if I have, I definitely wouldn't shoot it. And it's not because I'm a foreigner. I'm just quite firm on not shooting things,' I explained. 'Not even clay pigeons. So there.'

Tobias diffused the situation, announcing – through Georgina – that he couldn't bear lies.

'One wonders if boys are worth the trouble, darlings,' added Indie as she stretched out like a black cat on her bed and put her feet on the wall.

'This one doesn't wonder. I *know* they're not worth the trouble,' Star said as she braided her hair in front of the mirror.

'Oh, shut up, Star, you boring little child of a drugged-out has-been. You're just jealous of Calypso because she's got Freddie and you're too much of a freak to have a decent boyfriend.' Honey sneered from the windowsill where she was blowing out smoke.

What new hyper-reality was this? I couldn't believe that Honey of all people had come to *my* defence. Especially when I didn't even need rescuing. Besides, Star could have any boy she wanted.

Not that Star was bothered by Honey's slur on her pulling prowess. She merely picked up the Febreze and sprayed Honey's bum. 'Unlike you, when it comes to boys, I *choose* to refuse à la mo. Remind me, have you ever even had a proper boyfriend?'

Honey turned around to face us. I could physically feel her face throbbing with the indignity of the slight.

'Of course I have,' Honey insisted. 'Boys go mad for me.'

'Yes, yes, yes, darling, we know you're a slapper. You pull anyone in the least bit titled, regardless of whether they're even fit. But have you ever had an *actual* boyfriend?'

I could be wrong, but I was almost certain Honey hesitated before she said, 'Loads.'

'Oh really? Name them,' Indie said, a wide grin on her face.

'More like shame them,' Star added, laughing. 'Who'd go out with *you*?'

Suddenly the florescent lights went on. 'What's this?' Miss Bibsmore hissed from the doorway. 'You move that bin, Miss O'Hare, and git back to yer own room.'

'That is soooo unfair,' Honey fumed. I spotted Siddhartha peeking in the room and waved at him to bugger off.

'Unfair was made to fare,' replied Miss Bibsmore with a cackle. Then she turned to see what I was waving at and came face-to-face with Honey's Buddhist.

'What's this, then?' she asked, poking her stick at Siddhartha.

'My security guard,' Honey responded irritably.

Miss Bibsmore looked well cross. 'Your flaming what?' she railed. Even her fluffy dog slippers looked cross.

'Daddy thinks someone might be trying to kidnap me,' Honey replied casually.

'And what's that got to do with this fellow in a sari, then?' Miss Bibsmore wanted to know.

'He's a Buddhist monk, you ignoramus!' Honey said through clenched teeth.

'Ignorant, am I? Well leastways, no one's trying to kidnap me.'

'As if,' Honey muttered. Then she turned to us. 'Laters, peasants, I'm off to bed!' But as she went to squeeze past Miss Bibsmore, she was blocked by our house spinster's stick.

'Not so fast, Miss O'Hare. Rules is rules. No gentleman callers in the dorm.'

'Move aside, you mad old loon, or I'll have Siddhartha meditate you out of existence.'

Miss Bibsmore's stick continued to block Honey's exit. I know it's hard to imagine that a woman in a flannelette nightie and fluffy dog slippers can look fearsome, but Miss Bibsmore pulled it off. I was genuinely scared.

Honey sighed heavily. 'Listen, you bog ignorant chav, he's *not* a gentleman caller, he's a nonviolent licensed Buddhist security person.'

'I don't care if he's a reincarnated canary, Madam High and Mighty. He's got no business in a girls' dormitory innit. It's not proper, specially with a princess present an' all. I'm going to have to report this to Sister Constance, I am!'

Honey looked down on our dumpy little hunched house spinster in her grubby robe and dog slippers. 'Sister Constance has been fully informed about the threats made against my person. Now stand aside or I shall have Siddhartha deal with you.'

I don't suppose I was the only one wondering how a nonviolent Buddhist would deal with a fierce house spinster with a stick. Meditating her out of existence seemed a bit unlikely.

'Sort her out, Siddhartha,' Honey ordered, and next thing, Siddhartha produced a bronze cylinder on a stick from his robes and starting spinning it and chanting.

'Oh my God, he's got a gun!' Indie shrieked.

We all hit the floor, apart from Honey, Siddhartha and Miss Bibsmore, who brought her stick down on Siddhartha's prayer wheel. Honey screamed. I think I might have too, and then Indie pushed the panic button.

'Oh, lovely,' Star joked above the wail of the sirens. 'We've just summoned the police.'

Miss Bibsmore wasn't finished with Honey's Buddhist, though. She's quite the master of the ancient art of stickery, so I don't think anyone was surprised to see her whack Siddhartha over the head. Siddhartha lifted up his robes and legged it down the corridor to Miss Bibsmore's cries of, 'That's right, you big chicken in yer girlie frock. Cluck, cluck, cluck.'

It was all very undignified, and I suspect a severe blow to the credibility of Buddhist security guards everywhere.

The panic alarm was still blaring and Honey was still screaming when the police finally arrived.

'Alright, Sarge, it's just the O'Hare girl again,' one of the bobsters said into his walkie-talkie thingamee. 'We got a bloke outside in an orange sari an' all. Says he's from some Buddhist defence team sent to guard her from kidnappers, over.'

We heard a great deal of chuckling from the other end.

I know how the sarge felt. We all had to stuff our mouths with our duvets to stop chortling. The alarm was finally turned off, and Miss Bibsmore led the officers of the law to Sister's office, dragging Honey with her by the ear.

'Aren't you glad you came to England to go to school?' Star asked as she dove under the covers with me.

THIRTEEN

The Sword of Damocles

E ven though we were up most of the night chatting about Honey's Latest Prank, we all woke up at the first bell. After breakfast, chapel and room inspection, we loped off to English with Ms Topler. English being a core subject of the curriculum, we all had to do it. Which meant Star and I got to sit together. On top of each desk was a copy of *How to Pass Your Exams (And Enjoy Yourself)*.

I sat next to Star, who was decorating her booklet with some sort of musical score. I tried to read the booklet, which recommended taking breaks from study to walk the dog. What dog? I didn't even have a dog. I shut the book and set about a more disciplined and constructive activity: seeing how long I could go without writing *I love Freds* on my pencil case.

Star must have sensed my love battle because she looked up from her musical score and drew a heart on my hand in permanent marker. Then she added an *L* in the middle. Presumably it was intended to signify Loser rather than Love.

I snatched the marker off her and was about to draw a heart with an arrow through it on Star's hand when Ms Topler walked in. She was wearing an appallingly creepy pink floral dress with a pink cable-knit cardigan. Even her shoes were pink. They were those horrendous plastic ones that make a nauseating squelchy sound as you walk. Poor old dear, no wonder she's never found love and has to look to tragic cases like Thomas Hardy for comfort.

'Good morning, girls,' she trilled.

We all stood. 'Good Morning, Miss Topler, and may God bless you,' we chanted in the tone of worshipful respect which Saint Augustine's girls are famous for.

After a perfunctory '*In nomine patras, et filie et spiritus sancti,*' Miss Topler began jumping up and down as if she needed to do a wee. Then she clapped her hands together. 'Before we get under way on our term's work, I have a very exciting announcement to make.'

I thought she was going to say something mind-numbing, like how much fun she'd had with the metaphysical poets over the break. She always goes on about metaphysical poets when we all know they took vast amounts of narcotic drugs and hardly ever finished their poems. Whenever you point out blindingly obvious facts like this to Ms Topler, though, she showers you in blues.

But as it turned out, the metaphysical poets couldn't have been further from her mind. No, her announcement was worse than the worst metaphysical poem.

She clapped her hands, and like a guillotine falling on

my neck, she said, 'Calypso Kelly's essay, "My Family and Utter Madness," has been short-listed for the National Under Sixteens Essay Competition.'

Then she started the class off on a round of applause.

'Breathe,' Star told me as I swooned – and it wasn't even a fake swoon. In fact, it was very nearly a real faint!

'Breathe,' Star repeated. You know things are bad when you have to be reminded to do basic things like breathe.

'In, out, breathe, breathe!' Star urged as my head hit the desk with a thud.

'Is something the matter with our little heroine?' Ms Topler asked excitedly. I lifted my head as she strode towards me like a tall pink meringue. 'Oh, my giddy aunt,' I muttered. 'My life is over. If you have any *amore* for me whatsoever you'll kill me now, Star. Use a compass, a pencil, just shove it in my aura or aorta or whatever it is that makes you bleed to death. Please, Star, I beg of you.'

Ms Topler looked concerned.

'She's just overcome,' Star said. 'She often becomes a danger to herself when she's excited. I might take her out for a bit of air, if that's okay?'

Ms Topler concurred, harbouring the insane illusion that a bit of air was going to make things okay.

After Star had led me down the corridor, she gave me a hug. 'Don't worry. I'm sure you won't *win*.'

'But you told me last term that you were sure I *would* win.'

'I just said that so you'd enter,' she told me, grinning

broadly. 'It's an essay competition for people who've experienced great tragedy in their lives. *Great* tragedy! That's hardly *you*, Calypso.'

'But you told me last term that it *was!*' I said hotly. 'You said that Bob and Sarah's split was traumatic and tragic.'

'No, I didn't!' she argued. 'You've got a life of bliss and wonderfulness. You get to go back to LA and drive around in golf carts, and your parents aren't drug-addled rockers who can't remember your name.'

I glared at her. 'I assure you that you most certainly did urge me to enter. In fact I don't think saying you used strong-armed emotional force would be too far off the mark.'

'Well, maybe I did. But darling, I only did it for your own good.'

'It's not good to be murdered by your parents!'

'You're overreacting,' Star insisted.

'No, I am not. My essay will be published and Bob and Sarah will read about how totally insane they are!'

'What do you mean?'

Sometimes Star can be remarkably stupid and forgetful. I was starting to feel I'd get a more reasoned conversation from Tobias. 'You told me to write about the effect their breakup had on me!'

'So?'

'Well, one naturally uses a bit of artistic license to bring out the, you know, tragedy and pathos of one's situation.'

'Oh, does one?' she mocked.

'I just wrote about how crazy Bob and Sarah are – you know the regressing thing with Sarah; Bob's self-obsession with his Big One; and then I sort of inflated the whole drama for artistic effect.'

Star looked horrified. 'But they're so in love.'

'They weren't so in love then. They were separated, Star. Sarah was calling me Boojie and Bob was being distant and arrogant.'

'Bugger,' my friend exclaimed. 'Let's pray they don't buy the paper that day.' By the way she looked at me, I knew she had realised the full horror of my predicament.

When we went back to class, Ms Topler informed me of my reprieve. None of the essays would be published until after the judging, which was after half term. Phew, phew and double algebra phew.

My next class was double Greek, and we were subjected to a lecture on Damocles – who demonstrated the precariousness of happiness by making the chief sandal wearer of Ancient Greece sit under a sword dangling from a single hair. I don't know if that was ironic, but it was unnerving hearing about Damocles and his sword when I had one of my own hanging above me.

FOURTEEN

When Good Fantasies Go Bad

Damocles and his sword fear was long forgotten by Saturday afternoon, after classes ended. I was off to see Freds in Windsor! Despite his worrying txt the previous Sunday, nothing had 'come up,' and our rendezvous was going ahead as planned. I even attempted a celebratory cartwheel in our room, but my freakishly long legs got tangled in the curtains and the whole shooting match came tumbling down.

Luckily all Indie did was tickle me until I almost peed my pants and had a couple of her security guys re-hang the curtains.

Freds had been relatively quiet during the week. I'd tortured myself over Freds' lack of txts privately, but I didn't dare say anything in case it set Star off on her rant about boys taking up valuable creative brain space. Also, I'd been sufficiently distracted writing lyrics for Star and

Indie, which meant coming up with loads of words that
rhymed with 'angst' and 'anger.'

I'd taken a taxi into Windsor with Arabella and Clemmie, who, judging by their outfits, were out on the pull
big-time. They waited with me outside the taxi drop-off
place where I was rendezvousing with Freds.

'I hope he brings some fit friends,' Clemmie said as we
huddled under the awning.

'I told him I was coming in with you, so I'm sure he'll
bring someone,' I told her as we watched our bare legs go
blue with cold. I wish tights weren't so uncool. I know I
could have worn jeans, but I'd worn jeans last time I saw
Freds. Oh the sheer merde-arama of true love.

I'd actually asked Freds to bring a couple of mates along
to amuse Clems and Bells so I could be alone with him. I
hadn't seen him since the Scottish Fiasco as Star was now
referring to my trip to wildest Kiltland. She kept giving me
her impersonation of his disappointed looks, which had
everyone apart from me lying on the floor and kicking
their legs in the air with mirth. Now, 'mirth' is a good
word. Loads of words rhyme with 'mirth.'

Freddie arrived bang on time looking gorgeous. Hah! And
true to his word, he'd brought Malcolm and another boy.

'This is Orlando,' he said, introducing a fit guy I'd heard
of but never met. He was semi-famous in a school chat
room sort of way for being the 18th Lord of Hunte, a
famous DJ on the public school circuit, and for running
a Web site about Sloanes. It was meant to be a piss-take of

Sloaney values and dress, but loads of people (like Honey) took it tragically seriously. Orlando was wearing a really un-Sloaney Saville Row suit with a rugby jersey underneath and frayed white tennis shoes.

'You're looking blindingly beautiful today, Calypso,' Malcolm remarked, which made everyone muffle chortles. Apart from Freds, who stood by sullenly. Freds has been suspicious of Malcolm and me since last term, when I'd got stuck in the rain trying to climb the wall at Eades in the middle of the night. I was trying to get to Freds, but everything got muddled when I was caught in Malcolm's room in his robe while my clothes dried. Anyway, I think it's feverishly touching that Fred is so jealous, even though of course he doesn't need to be. As fit as Malcolm is, he's blatantly keen on Indie.

'So everything's cool with your parents now, then?' Malcolm asked.

'I told you about their marriage blessing, McHamish,' Freddie chided, nudging Malcolm, who nudged him back. Then that turned into a nudge-fest as Malcolm replied, 'Yaah, but I thought you were lying, didn't I?'

Freds and I both rolled our eyes, and Freds squeezed me into his chest and kissed the top of my head. Then he suggested we go for pizza. I nodded, and Freds told the others we'd catch them later as he put his arm around my shoulders and pulled me down the lane.

'That's okay, we'll join you,' Malcolm said, trailing after us with the others in tow.

Even though I was looking forward to time alone with Freds, neither of us could really say anything without appearing rude. Just the same, I thought to myself, Freds could have at least given me a significant look – a look that said 'oh how I wish it were just you and me, Calypso, darling.'

But he didn't.

All six of us set off down the cobbled lanes, slipping in the sludgy snow and catching one another. I slipped a few more times than necessary so Freds could catch me. Oh winter love, I love it.

At our pizza haunt we all sat at a big table in the corner. Freds pulled a seat out for me and sat next to me. He has so much savoir-faire.

Arabella was blatantly flirting with Malcolm, which was pointless given the fatal attraction Indie held for him. Meanwhile, Clems was fluttering her eyelashes in Orlando's direction. I asked Freds how Kev was.

'Brilliant,' Freds said tonelessly as he scanned the menu.

'Oh!' I remarked, moving closer to him and pretending to scan the menu – as if my pizza choice seriously mattered. I always have Hawaiian and Freds always has pepperoni – it's our thing.

'Why, what's up?' he asked, finally sensing that all was not well in Calypso's Very Own Fantasyland.

'Nothing,' I fibbed because I was hoping to hear tales of Kev's broken heart. In Calypso's Very Own Fantasyland, I had imagined Freds pleading for my intervention for the sake of his best friend's health. Nothing would give me more joy than to reunite Kev and Star so we could be the perfect foursome we once were.

Even though Star hadn't actually mentioned him since she announced dumping him, I felt sure she must still *like* him. I mean, seriously. He did *everything* she said. And he was fit and he could fence like a demon. All her talk about boys being a pain was just that, talk. That's what I'd talked myself into believing anyway. 'Just, well, Star told me they broke up, and I thought Kev might have said something.'

'Yaah, probably for the best. Things had run their course there, I gather,' Freds answered.

'Run their *what*?' I blurted.

'Their course,' he repeated, looking at me like I was a right bonkermaniac.

If I could have done that thing the girl did in *The Exorcist* and swivelled my head around and around and around, that's what I would have done. Instead, my eyes popped out of my head and fell on the floor – well virtually.

'Star has GCSEs to focus on,' he added. And then he looked at me as if he were noticing me for the very first time and said, 'You've got your GCSEs too, haven't you?'

'So?' I asked, wondering what on earth he was on about. Who wants to talk about feverishly dreary GCSEs when there are lips to be kissed and lovely sticky-outy hair to be stroked?

'Well, I'm just saying, you probably have a lot of, erm, time constraints.'

I had no idea where his head was. I know boys are from a different planet, but this was *different* different. There was no room to faint in the crowded restaurant, so I slumped on the table and snored. That at least made him touch my hair, although it was more of a ruffle – sort of like you might give a dog.

Having ruined my lovely hairstyle, he looked at the others and asked, 'Shall we just order three large mixed and split them?'

'Not for me,' Malcolm said, looking at me as he pushed his chair back. 'I might get going, actually. Good to see you girls,' he said vaguely, and then he just walked out of the café.

It was peculiar the way he backed out of the café, still looking at me as if trying to convey something. I presumed he wanted news of Indie or something, but he only had to ask.

Orlando told Freds to go ahead and order three large mixed anyway. Then the two of them started chatting about Eades stuff, and I was left to join in a conversation with Clemmie and Bells about our rabbits. I know they're my friends, and rabbits are adorable, but Clems and Arabella and me – well, we see each other every day. Actually, I share a room with Clemmie every night. Love rabbits though I do, I didn't need to come all the way into Windsor to chat about them. I came to pull Freds!

FIFTEEN

Pi-Squared Shockarama

It wasn't until after the pizzas were finished that we finally got a chance to be alone. Freds took control, saying to Orlando, 'We're off now, Hunte, see you back at school.'

I loved hearing him say *we*. It made me feel warm and wanted. It was a shame Hunte was too busy being love-bombed by Arabella and Clems to notice.

I snuggled under Freds' arm as he chucked some money down and we set off into the snow. Outside I pulled his arm around me even more tightly. 'I'm freezing,' I told him, fluttering my lashes seductively. At least, it would have been seductive if they hadn't been glued together from all the mascara I was wearing. As it was I had to pretend I had something in my eye, and Freds dabbed at me with his handkerchief.

'Do you want my jacket?' he asked, pulling away and removing his cashmere coat. 'No, you flaming idiot! I want your arms around me,' I screamed inside.

Then he looked down at my legs and said, 'You're blue. Why aren't you wearing tights, Calypso?'

What was he, my grandmother? 'Oh, I don't feel the cold,' I lied.

'I thought you Californians were all sun-worshipping surf queens,' he teased.

'We *do* get snow in California you know,' I told him. 'It's only an hour's drive from LA.'

He laughed. And then, just as I started to feel perfect and blissful, he shoved his hands in the pockets of his chinos and said, 'So, you've got a lot on, what with your GCSEs and your tournament in Italy.'

'I wish you were coming to Italy,' I told him. 'Is there anyway you could tag along?'

He laughed as if I'd only been joking, which I found très vexing. He was a prince after all, and he wasn't doing GCSEs. Why couldn't he come to Italy?

Then he looked all serious again. 'I know Billy's training *really* hard.'

'So are Portia and I,' I told him. 'Every lunch hour we're en guarding our heads off in the salle.'

'That's what I thought. I really support you, which is why I want you to know I'd completely understand if you wanted a break.'

I felt cold now. Ice cold. 'A break from what?' I asked, as if I didn't know what the word 'break' meant.

He looked at his shoes. Why do boys do that when they're going to say something awful? To change the mood

I added, 'I wouldn't mind a break from this weather. Snuggle up to me,' I said, not wanting the conversation to continue any further.

Freds ignored me. 'Well, us. I mean you and me. I just don't want you to feel, you know . . .'

His voice trailed off as he looked me in the eye.

'No, I don't,' I told him. 'I don't know what you're banging on about, actually.'

'I just don't want you to feel like you have to hang out with me when you need to focus on other things like fencing. I know how hard you worked to get onto the international team, and I don't want you to think of us as an obligation.'

I breathed out. Phew. He didn't want to break up at all, he was just feeling insecure and I was just being paranoid. 'You're not an obligation,' I reassured him. Then I gave him a playful nudge, hoping to nudge him into taking his hands out of his pockets and putting them around me again where they belonged. 'You're a pleasure.'

'You know what I mean, Calypso. Portia and Billy are taking time out, and Kev and Star and . . .'

'We're not musketeers, Freddie,' I said. 'We don't have to follow our mates as if they were a conga line.'

He didn't even smile. Actually he didn't even look at me. He went back to fixating on his shoes, which as far as I could tell looked perfectly unremarkable. 'I'm just saying I know you have a lot on, so if you, well, you know, want to have a break or something, I'd understand.'

I bent down and looked up into his face so I could look him in the eye. 'Are you trying to tell me something, Freddie?' My heart was pounding. He looked more awkward than I'd ever seen him. The next seconds of silence were painful. I closed my eyes, terrified that he was about to dump me. But he ended my agony by putting his arms around me. He kissed me gently on the lips. I felt so warm and perfect inside again. Everything was fine! Well, I did a pretty good job of convincing myself that everything would be all right anyway. I pretended the awful bit where he'd mentioned a break was down to insecurity and his honourable intentions to give me more time for my endeavours.

When we stopped kissing and looked into each other's eyes, Freds was smiling. So I smiled too. 'Let's put you in a taxi,' he said, kissing my frozen nose.

I was still floating on a turbulent sea of confusion ten minutes later as I turned into the lane that led to Saint Augustine's. Now I knew what it felt like to float above your pain. Everything was okay, I told myself. Freds was just having an insecurity complex. But as I watched the deodorising cardboard tree hanging from the rear-view mirror, nothing really felt okay. The deodorising tree wasn't deodorising the taxi, and I wasn't doing a good job of feeling on top of the world.

It wasn't until I entered the main building that I realised I had left Clems and Arabella in Windsor, breaking the school rule of go in threes, stay in threes, come back in threes. I was about to call them and apologise, but when I checked my phone, I noticed the time. Curfew was still two hours away. And I didn't need Mr Templeton to do that sum for me! I could have stayed two hours longer with Freds.

I called Clemmie and Arabella and apologised for leaving them. They said they were about to go to the cinema with Orlando and another friend of his, Yo. I couldn't help feeling that Freds should have taken *me* to the cinema. Talk about hitting the ground with a thud. It was pointless fainting, as there was no one around to notice.

As much as I kept telling myself that Freds' suggestion that I might want to take a break was motivated by honourable intentions, I couldn't shake the horrible gnawing in my stomach. I headed to the music wing in search of Indie and Star. Maybe writing some disaffected teen lyrics would make me feel better.

The music wing wasn't officially opened yet. That treat would come in two weeks when the plaque was finished. Star was privileged to have early access because her father had paid for it. It looked more like Abbey Road Recording Studios than a school music wing, probably because Star's father's platinum albums lined the walls of the lobby-ish area. As I wandered through the entrance corridor, I kept expecting a beautiful receptionist to dive out and offer me Evian. Even a few stoned roadies would not have seemed out of place. The only jarring note was an oil painting of Our Lady with a set of rosary beads.

I expected to find Star and Indie, but Malcolm was there as well. I don't know why I was so surprised to see him, given he'd snuck into Saint Augustine's last term.

'Ah, Calypso! At last. Champagne?' he asked, pulling a mini bottle of Veuve Clicquot out of the six-pack by his feet.

Drinking champagne and having a boy on the premises could lead to a suspension, but Malcolm looked so at home with Star's bass guitar around his neck that I forgot the risk we were all taking. I nodded my acceptance to the offer of champagne, even though I don't really like the stuff. I was in shock, really. A shock which was about to intensify by pi square when Malcolm uttered the impossible words, 'I daresay you need a drink after being dumped.'

SIXTEEN

Bonkeratus, Bonkeratum, Bonkerama

As it was, I did an actual faint and crumpled up at Malcolm's feet. I felt quite the Georgian lady – you know those 'gels' Miss Austen wrote about in such yawn-making detail. They do one of those swooney wooneys and the next minute, Darcy or some other git goes into feverish overdrive to bring the corseted lass around.

Back in the twenty-first century, I came to, looked up and saw Malcolm looking mildly curious rather than alarmed. He was preoccupied with easing the cork off the miniature champagne bottle.

Star and Indie helped me up, and Star gave me a cuddle. 'How dare he dump *you*!' she declared hotly.

'He didn't dump me,' I insisted. 'He hasn't dumped me!' I pointed at Malcolm. 'He's just being Scottish!'

All eyes turned to Malcolm, who had successfully removed the cork and was now giving it a sniff and wrinkling his nose. He turned to me and winced before saying, 'Sorry, I appear to have set the veritable cat out amongst the veritable whatsits.'

Malcolm stuck the straw in the miniature bottle and held it to my lips. Why was this mad loon of a boy always trying to shove alcohol down my neck?

'Drink deeply from the well of fizz, Calypso. In the words of Madame Bollinger, "I drink it when I am happy, I drink it when I am sad." Besides, you don't want to take anything I say seriously. I've probably got it all wrong. He was no doubt off to dump some other hapless girl and not your good self after all. Forget everything I said.'

I pushed the champagne away and roughly wiped a tear from my cheek. Malcolm hadn't got it wrong. Deep down I knew that. All that guff Freds had been burbling in Windsor about how he'd understand if I wanted to take a break. He had wanted to dump me all along. He'd just bottled out because he didn't want me to cry, or make a scene, or do something disappointing.

'If you ask me, he was a bit wet for you anyway,' Malcolm remarked, sipping the champagne himself.

'I agree,' said Star. 'Wet as soggy gym socks. You're much better off without him.'

Star would say that. Operation Dumping Boys was going splendidly – well, in a reverse sort of way anyway.

'Better off without whom?' my *bête noire*, Honey, asked

as she wandered into the studio wearing yet another slinky sundress. Her bony arms were covered in nicotine patches but she was still smoking a fag.

'Freds dumped Calypso,' Malcolm said, offering her a miniature.

'Poor lamb,' Honey said, taking the bottle. 'Here, have a nicotine patch, darling, they really give you a lift,' she offered, peeling one off her arm and slapping it on my forehead. Then she plonked herself down on the floor beside me and put her arm around my shoulder as if she really, really cared.

I didn't know what was worse. My despair that Freds didn't love me anymore or having Honey pretend to pity me. She blew a plume of smoke in my face, which made me cough, so she sprayed the air around me with Febreze, which made my eyes tear up. 'Poor, sad little tragic Calypso. You must feel like utter dirt. You must feel as though your life's not worth living. You must feel like slashing your wrists or diving from the bell tower to your macabre and bloody death – or at least a coma. I know I would if I were you.'

'She's far better off without him,' Malcolm said stoutly, roughly snatching back the bottle of champagne he'd given Honey.

'I'm not better off without him, though,' I insisted. 'He's not a drip and he didn't actually dump me!' I carried on, my voice rising into a hysterical screech. Très unattractive, I know, but I was like one of those crazed women in films who have just had a horrible shock and need a good slap.

Honey slapped me hard across the face.

Then Star slapped Honey back even harder.

Malcolm must have wondered what kind of slappity-slap circus he'd entered, but he didn't show it. Not that I was thinking about Malcolm's feelings at the time. I was remembering Freds' good-bye kiss and how lovely and real it had felt. Oh God, it was all so confusing. Please God, let Malcolm be wrong. Freds loves me. He told me so.

Besides, Malcolm wasn't even one of Freds' mates. Malcolm was in the year above and made weird art movie thingies that Freds wasn't keen on. 'Malcolm's got it all wrong. It must have been a mistake,' I told everyone. 'Freds loves me.'

Honey snickered.

No one else looked convinced either.

'He's still wet,' Malcolm muttered as he swizzled the straw of his champagne.

Star agreed enthusiastically.

Sucking hard on her cigarette, Honey nodded. Blowing a series of artful smoke rings in my eyes, she said, 'Soz, darling' and sprayed me with Febreze.

I didn't rise to their bait, though. *They* hadn't been there in Windsor in the snow when Freds kissed me good-bye. *They* couldn't grasp the true depth of his *je ne sais quoi* or his savoir-faire. Okay, so he wasn't exactly the life of the party, but he made me feel special, and without wanting to sound shallow, he was heir to the throne. Every girl in the world worshipped him – apart from Star.

'And what's with his hair?' Malcolm asked, shaking his head. 'You should see the pots of gel in his room. Has it delivered by the lorry load every Monday, the vain git.'

'Freds doesn't use gel,' I blurted, because everyone knows that boys who use gel are très, très tragic.

Malcolm shook his head. 'You never did find your way into his room, did you, Calypso? For if you had, well. Gel Central, I'm afraid.'

Star giggled. 'I know, he looks like such a chav.'

Indie giggled. 'Gel is soooo sad. You'd think one of his lackeys would tell him.'

Even Honey laughed – well, as best she could.

I looked around at the faces of my friends and Honey. I wanted to be alone with Star and tell her how terrible I felt, but I knew she'd just say stuff like how I was better off without him. This scenario was, after all, just what she wanted. But then she surprised me by announcing, 'Listen, though, seriously, we can't allow this to happen. Freddie can't be allowed to dump Calypso.'

I could have kissed her! No wonder I loved Star so much. To quote from some addled Latin text we were translating, she is most definitely the *ne plus ultra* of girlfriends, the alpha and omega of friends.

When she came over and hugged me, I hugged her back so hard she made a squeaking sound. Everything would be okay now.

'No Saint Augustine's girl has ever been dumped. We're the ones who do the dumping,' she told me.

'But he didn't actually *dump* me,' I reminded her.

'Okay, so he chickened out, but according to Malcolm, that was his plan.'

I looked over at Malcolm, who shrugged and nodded in the affirmative.

'It's an immutable fact, my darling bestest friend in the world,' Star said to me. 'No boy, not even a prince, has ever dumped a Saint Augustine's girl. Ever.'

Just then Georgina walked in with Tobias. What was this, Humiliation Central? 'Apparently there was some incident of a Stowe boy dumping some girl in the sixties,' she said, clearly already *au fait* with my shame. Maybe Freds had pasted posters declaring his dumping intentions over Windsor.

'Typical,' Malcolm sneered. 'What do you expect from Stowe?'

'Sister Constance will flip when she hears one of her girls has been dumped,' Honey said gleefully.

Star gave her a warning look. 'Do you want a wrist burn, Honey?'

Honey grabbed her thin little wrists in fear.

'No one is telling Sister. Freds hasn't *officially* dumped Calypso *yet*,' Star said, the word 'yet' going through my heart like a dagger. 'There's still time to save the situation if we act quickly.'

Georgina gave me Tobias to hug. He was wearing a fetching little black Prada jumper and some vintage Vivienne Westwood bondage trousers, teemed with workman's earmuffs - presumably to protect his ears from the noise of Star and Indie's music. 'Tobias said you're not to worry, darling, we'll sort it out.'

Just then I heard my txt alert going off.

Honey grabbed my bag off the chair and pulled out my phone. '"Soz and all that, but I think we should take a break! I'll call later, F,"' she read. Then she made a really sad, pitying face that made her pumped-up collagen-enhanced lips loll around her chin.

Star snatched my mobile from her and scanned the message. 'Bugger. What an absolute jerk,' she said, chucking the phone to me in disgust.

'The txt dump is a low blow,' Malcolm said. 'Even for a wet prince lathered in chav gel.'

I read the txt myself, wanting it say something other than what Honey and Star had read. But it didn't.

Soz and all that, but I think we should take a break! I'll call later, F

It was true. I had been dumped by the heir to the throne. What's more, I had been dumped by txt, an instrument designed for flirting and sending lovely messages to friends! All the confusion I had felt earlier drained out of me as I read and reread the stark cruelty of the words.

All I felt now was outrage and anger. I looked up at the concerned faces of the others and stood up in fury. 'Right. He's toast.'

Malcolm raised his bottle in the air. 'Here's to toasting the little wet!' I know that it wasn't the time to be thinking such things, but hearing him call Freds 'the little wet' suddenly made me realise that Malcolm was actually quite fit.

Georgina, Honey, Indie and Star all grabbed a bottle each and clunked them against Malcolm's.

'Toast!' everyone declared.

Then Indie turned to me and said, 'You could always perform The Counter Dump. A girl at Cheltenham Ladies had to do The Counter Dump once – the guy was destroyed! He never pulled again.'

SEVENTEEN

The Mechanics of The Counter Dump

How many teenagers can you fit in a dorm room built to accommodate three girls? Forty-two, that's how many – the entire Year Eleven. There were girls on ledges, girls on cupboards, even girls in the bath in the en suite – all of them wearing the hideous plastic bead bracelets of Enterprise Initiative.

By that evening, I had become a cause celeb, only not in a good way like Nelson Mandela or that woman who is trying to bring down the cruel regime in Burma. No, my name had become associated with shame. The word was out. Girls, teachers, nuns and house spinsters were all aghast that one of their own, a Saint Augustine's girl, had been so brutally dumped.

Walking down corridors, you could hear snatches of conversation like, 'I just don't understand how it could have happened,' and 'I heard he uses *gel*.'

I was as much at a loss to understand my dumping as

they were. I had no answers, only questions. But all I really wanted was a solution, and that's what Indie promised she had.

'Right. The main thing is to restore honour to our school, right?' she asked.

'And to Calypso,' Star added.

'*Especially* to Calypso,' Indie agreed, smiling sweetly at me. 'The skillful execution of The Counter Dump is based on Calypso getting Freds in a lather over her again and then just as he realises that life without her isn't worth living, she dumps him.'

'Here, here!' the room cheered.

'Believe me, I've witnessed a Counter Dump firsthand. It will make Freds feel like a pig's dinner for the rest of his life. He will never pull another girl again.'

Everyone seemed thrilled by this outcome. I mean, I know he dumped me, but a pig's dinner? I don't know that I'd wish that on anyone – not that I have the slightest clue what pig's dinners consist of.

'Seriously, he will never pull again,' Indie repeated for dramatic effect.

An image of Freds as a Lady Haversham character flashed through my mind and I giggled, which set everyone else off. As I looked around at the faces of the girls perched and squeezed into our tiny room, I couldn't help but be touched. It was a coming together of the school such as I'd never witnessed. Even Honey – who was perched companionably with Polo Central on the wardrobe – thought The Counter Dump was the only way for me to regain my dignity. I was shocked that Honey felt I had any dignity in need of restoration, given she'd spent the last four years trying to strip me of it.

'Calypso?' Indie asked.

Portia nudged me from my musings and I realised a speech was required, so I blurted, 'I want to see Freds grovel.'

The girls started clapping and banging their legs on whatever they could. Spurred by this show of *belle esprit*, I continued, 'I want to rinse him good and proper. Horrible boy, hiding his nasty cruel streak under such lovely sticky-outy hair and kissable lips.'

More cheers went up and my emotions were swept along with the fervour of the crowd. Maybe Freds *should* feel like a pig's dinner, at least for a bit. I certainly hoped he'd never pull again. That would teach him.

'Speech! Speech!' everyone cried.

Feeling rather like Cicero on a good day, I began, 'Boys and their enormous egos. Who does he think he is? Apart from the prince of the United Bollocky Pollicky Kingdom, I mean. If we let him get away with dumping me, well, it will be open season on all of us!'

The roar of the crowd rivalled any Roman mob. It was a wonder we weren't being plagued by house spinsters left, right and centre.

Star clapped her hands flamenco-style to call the meeting to order. 'Right, so basically the honour not just of Calypso, but of the entire school is at stake! Agreed?

There was more banging of feet on the floor, the sides of wardrobes, cupboards, walls or baths as everyone showed their support. Then Star said, 'Indie has suggested that Calypso bring Freds to his knees by performing The Counter Dump, a manoeuvre guaranteed to knock the stuffing out of the most egotistical of boys.'

Georgina covered poor Tobias's ears – as a soft toy, he doesn't like talk about knocking the stuffing out of things.

'How dare he dump me by txt,' I said – for like the thousandth millionth time since receiving his horrible txt.

'At least now you can see him for the enormous idiot he is,' Star pointed out. 'I told you that you should dump him after that fiasco with the fake cold in Scotland,' Star told me.

'And I told you that I hate being told "I told you so,"' I replied.

Star blushed. 'Sorry, darling. Think of it as fodder for your lyrics,' she advised more gently, chucking me her lipgloss. 'We'll all help you avenge your honour.'

'Don't be so culturally insensitive,' Honey argued hotly. 'Think of Calypso, poor love; she's American, and everyone knows they don't know what honour is.'

Star took off her shoe and threw it at Honey. But our *bête noire* caught it adroitly, looked at the label, screwed up her nose job and chucked it right back.

I know I should have felt insulted by what Honey said, but the horror of it all was, I was worried she might be right! I really wasn't in the least bit worried about my bloody honour, or the school's honour for that matter. I wanted to sob uncontrollably into my pillow and then pretend it was Freds and thump it.

'Indie's right, though. The only thing to do is seduce him all over again, and then when he's down on his knees with love for you, txt him a dump message,' Fenella said, without looking up from the copy of *Horse and Hound* she was flicking through.

'I didn't seduce him in the first place, though – I trounced him at sabre,' I explained.

'What's sabre?' Perdita asked.

'It's like something you do with swords, only not on horseback, darling,' Georgina explained.

'Huh,' Perdita nodded. 'Like water polo, you mean?'

'Exactly,' Star agreed, rolling her eyes at me.

'So this seduction business, how do we go about it, precisely?' Portia asked. 'No offence, but Calypso is no Mata Hari.'

'I think we'll need a decoy,' Honey suggested. 'Perhaps I could pull Freds to distract him and . . .'

'He said he'd call,' Portia reminded her calmly with the sort of poise only a girl who can trace her title back generations can possess. Like Star, most of the rest of the world just wants to throw shoes at Honey. 'Let's presume he'll be true to his word and call Calypso.'

I grabbed my mobile and checked it was on. 'But what should I say when he does call?' I asked. 'If he actually does call, I mean,' I added, as doubts engulfed me.

'Whatever you do, you must not answer it,' Indie advised sternly.

'I can't do that,' I told her. It was true, I'm not one of those people that can call-screen. I go doo-lally with curiosity.

Star took the phone from me and started pressing buttons. 'I've put it on mute and on mute it will stay,' she told me firmly, tossing it back to me.

'Do you think he will leave a message, though?' I asked.

'No,' Perdita said knowledgably. 'Boys don't ever leave unpleasant messages. He might just say he'll call back, or see you at the next polo match or ask you to call him.'

'On Saturday,' said Star. 'When Calypso and posse head into Windsor, we should arrange to meet Malcolm and get him to bring his entourage. That way, when Freds sees you, you'll be surrounded by friends and fit boys.'

It did sound like a cool plan, but was Malcolm the ideal decoy? 'What if he doesn't care that I'm with Malcolm's entourage and a posse of girls?' I asked, because really, and I know this is sinfully self-centred, I wanted him to care so much that he'd sob at the sight of me and beg me to take him back. Of course I would spurn him, but still I wanted to know he cared first.

Star chortled, 'Oh darling, I do love you for being so naive when it comes to boys. Freds may not be deep, but his ego is enormous. He'll notice you with Malcolm. Remember how jealous he was when you accidentally climbed into Malcolm's room at Eades that night in the rain?'

'But he knows Malcolm and Indie are practically an item. He'll just presume I'm a cling-on.'

Indie looked shocked. 'Since when have Malcolm and moi been an item?'

I blinked so hard with confusion I began to get a migraine. 'Erm, forever?'

'Are you mad?' she replied – though clearly the question was meant to be rhetorical. 'Malcolm's cool but . . .' She shook her braids and said, 'Portia, you explain.'

EIGHTEEN

It Was All Très, Très, Très Befuddling

All forty-two girls were silent as Portia rolled her eyes and said, 'Indie's pulled Tarquin.'

Georgina threw Tobias at her. 'Tobias can't bear secrets. Why didn't you tell us?' she asked furiously.

The rest of the room muttered their displeasure. Indie kissed Tobias on the nose and threw him back to Georgina. 'Because you and Star were banging on about how we should stop being so boy-obsessed.'

'Has no one in this school heard of the word *proportion*?' Star groaned.

'I thought you and Malcolm were an item, too,' Perdita added.

'Buggery slops,' Star cursed. 'Anyway, everyone, let's stay on message. *When* Freds approaches you, seething with jealousy, you have to be really carefree and breezy. Charming but distant, you know, sort of look at him and smile as if you can't quite remember who he is.'

'Don't be *too* obvious, though,' Georgina warned as she brushed Tobias's fur. 'I mean, boys aren't that clever, but they usually know when they are being played.'

'That's true. Be a bit flirty without actually flirting, if you know what I mean,' Arabella suggested. 'You know, twirl your hair, pout your lips and titter gaily.'

'What? Freds will think I'm mad if I start tittering gaily, or tittering in any way for that matter. And as for pouting and twirling my hair, well . . . he'll think my madness is out of hand and call for the asylum lorry to take me to an island of loons.'

'She's right,' agreed Honey. Then she looked at me with big blue sad-eyed pity. 'Poor, poor tragically butch Calypso. I'll help you learn the art of seduction, darling,' she advised in a mildly threatening sort of way. 'Seduction is my middle name.'

The awful thing was, Seduction probably *was* Honey's middle name. After all, her sister Poppy's middle name was Minxy-Darling. I swear, Minxy-Darling. No wonder they're the twisted sisters.

'The thing is,' advised Indie seriously, 'is that you have to get him to want you back really, really badly.'

'Desperately badly,' Bells added.

'And then when he thinks he's won you back, you have to dump him from a great height,' Indie explained.

'And destroy his hopes and dreams of ever being loved again,' Honey concluded as she admired her reflection in her Chanel compact.

'Can any of the rest of us pull him, I mean once The Counter Dump is over?' Clems piped up.

We were all laughing loudly when Miss Bibsmore entered, her dressing gown billowing. She was in a furious mood. 'I've been listening to yous girls from behind the door an' all. No one's pulling that little sod again, do you hear?' she railed, waving her stick around the room, almost knocking girls' heads off. 'Treating a lovely girl like Miss Kelly worse than you'd treat a mongrel dog. All the teachers and nuns are behind you on this an' all. You mark my words. You girls have got to teach this cheeky pup that a Saint Augustine's girl 'as pride innit. Boys like His Nibs aren't for the likes of ladies like yourselves. He'll be blacklisted by this school and no bones about it neither. I've got a good mind to recommend to Sister that we start a hate club like what we did for . . . well, never you mind about that.'

'A hate club.' Honey said the words like they were a dream come true. 'That would be soooo cool. We could have badges and a Web site and plan attacks.'

'Yes, well, that sort of thing,' Miss Bibsmore conceded, clearly perturbed to be on the same team as Honey.

The bearded Miss Cribbe, our house spinster from last year, poked her head around the door. ''Ello, dearies, now don't be a stranger where I is concerned neither. If there's anything I can do to put His Nibs in his place, you just let me know.'

All the girls cheered and then the nuns appeared.

'And don't forget us old things up at the convent,' piped up little Sister Regina, her face crinkled with years of prayer and concern. 'We may not have had a great deal of experience

with boys, but we're all behind you on this. Sister Constance
has told us to lend you every support. Though I must say,
Freddie seemed like such a lovely young man when we met
him at the Nationals. A real gentleman he was.'

I was quite moved. It was all very touching if a little
daunting, the realisation that everyone was being so
supportive. I know I felt enraged with Freds, but was I
really up to performing The Counter Dump?

'I blame the parents, I do,' Miss Bibsmore told Sister
stoutly. 'Spoilt and pampered he is, like a prize bull.'

That set all of us off on a chortle jag again, which sent
girls tumbling off wardrobes and chests of drawers.

Miss Bibsmore waved her stick at us. 'Now there's nothing
to giggle at here, girls. The school's honour is at stake.'

Laughter aside, the bitter sadness of my situation came home
after everyone had gone back to their own rooms. I finally found
the bottle to answer Sarah and Bob's txt from yesterday asking about me, my school work and that cur of curs, Freddie.

School is totally pants but I'm bearing up. xxx C.
PS: Fred's fab and sends love.

I mean, I couldn't exactly tell them that Freds had
dumped me by txt, could I? Knowing Sarah and Bob, I bet
they would have set off in the car of shame, dragged him
from the comfort of his bed at Eades and given him one of
their really, really long lectures.

Just the same, writing that lie of lies about Freds
sending love made me cry myself to sleep.

NINETEEN

Snoozely Woozely Does It

I solved the mystery of my missing skirts Monday morning when Indie found them wedged behind the completely useless non-heat-radiating radiator in our room.

'Sebastian probably hid them there.' Clems giggled. But I couldn't feel cross about Sebastian as all my cross feelings were focused on Freds.

Down in the chaos of clashing dishes and chatter in the ref, Star waved us over to her table, where she'd saved us a bench. 'I called Malcolm this morning and he's totally on for Operation Counter Dump,' she told us as we sat down. 'We're all convening in Windsor on Saturday at two.'

'He's going to get a posse together of fit boys from his film club too,' Portia added. 'Tarkie told me.'

I imagined a hellish troop of pimpled film buffs in tight black clothes banging on about Federico Fellini and almost died with the dreariness of it all, but Indie was wriggling excitedly in her seat, so I didn't verbalise my doubts. Tarquin was fit enough, though – and a member of Malcolm's film club – so Indie was no doubt over the moonarama at the prospect of seeing him.

But my enthusiasm was somewhat diluted. First, I wasn't convinced that Freds would even show on Saturday. And second, even if he did show, I wasn't sure he'd be that devastated to see me with my posse chatting to Malcolm and his nerdy film club in their stupid tight black clothes.

But Star was on a mission. 'See, everything's going according to plan,' she told me, shoving a piece of croissant in my mouth so I couldn't argue.

After chapel and room inspection we made our way to maths, where Mr Templeton was eager to arouse our young minds with hard sums and amusing theorems. He actually talked like that.

'I've got something really exciting to stimulate those little grey cells of yours today, girls,' he told us as he rubbed his hands together like some Machiavellian priest of evil.

We tried to look spellbound and interested – or at least not about to expire from boredom - but it was très, très challenging.

'Yes, girls! It's my favourite subject, and I sincerely hope it will soon be yours. It's called trigonometry, or as our ancient Latin friends called it, *trigonometria*.'

I don't think I was the only girl in the class wondering what ancient Latin friends he or any of the rest of us had. I doubt he has any friends frankly, not with his tragic capacity for delusion.

Most of the class were either pocket-eating their breakfast, checking txts under their desks or writing whimsical things about boys on their stationery.

But Mr Templeton was undeterred. He banged on relentlessly, making up even more ridiculous words like 'sine,' 'cos' and some other thingameepiglets. I put my head on the desk for a nice little snoozy woozy. I hadn't slept well the night before because of all the Counter Dump issues.

The next thing I knew, a piece of chalk hit me on the head. I swear it practically decapitated me. If that's not against European Human Rights legislation, I don't know what is.

'Miss Kelly, were you asleep?' Mr Templeton asked.

Seriously, the man was the apex of all that is sadly mad about grown-ups. 'Of course I was asleep!' I blurted as I rubbed my sore little head.

How could anyone keep their eyes open with someone banging on about the measurement of triangles? I don't even like triangles. They're unnatural. Then again so is Mr Templeton.

Still it was my duty as a well-brought-up student to humour the horrible little man. So I said – ultra, ultra sweetly – 'Sorry, Mr Templeton. I was just having a nice little dream about sine, cos and the, erm, that other lovely trigonomonstic thingamee you were telling us about.'

Mr Templeton was not even mildly mollified by my excuse. 'Fine, then you'll have no trouble giving me three blues on the fascinating tables I was just explaining to everyone, will you?'

Seriously, those heady days when Pythagoras could hold a crowd spellbound with theorems and tricky sums were long gone, with no small thanks to teachers like Mr Templeton.

All in all it was a pretty blue week for me. Every time I tried to have a bit of a snooze in class, some sadistic teacher would slap a pile of blues on me.

I suppose it did distract me from thinking about Freds, who called me once a night. It took more willpower than I ever knew I had not to answer my phone. As predicted by the wise girls of Polo Central, though, he left no message. If I hadn't been so tired from practising for our trip to Florence with the national fencing team, I would have agonised over why he only bothered to call once a night. Did that mean he only thought of my poor broken heart once? Or was he being all dignified and decent and trying not to stalk me?

I would have liked him to call a hundred desperate times a day. I would have liked to hear him sobbing away disgracefully on my answer service. At least then I would know that my charms were powerful enough to bring a boy to tears. As it was, I just felt annoyed. Which is why I started writing songs.

I know it was just a first draft of my first song ever, but

by Friday I thought it was going quite magnifique, I really, really did. I was so tremulous with pride, I rushed to the music wing to share my opus with Indie and Star, whom I hoped would give my self-esteem that much-needed lift.

They took the pages from me, and Star read the lyrics out but without injecting any feeling into them whatsoever.

> He stole my heart with his sticky-outy hair
> and then he broke it in two, oooh, oooh.
> My heart is soooo broken and my mind's so confused,
> and I don't know what to dooo, oooh, ooh.
> If I wasn't afraid of getting more blues,
> I'd take my sabre and cut him in two,
> yes, that's exactly what I'd do! Oooh! Oooh!
> That's exactly what I'd do, ooooooooooooooh yaaaaaah.

Star and Indie said it was a good first effort, which was a bit underwhelming. Still, they had a go at writing the melody for it – if you can call the noise their band makes melodious.

Indie did a great job singing the lyrics though, which in my humble opinion sounded brilliant and feverishly meaningful. But Star said it wasn't long enough, and Indie suggested I might want to 'rework it a bit.'

'Or maybe even a lot,' added Star.

Like most rock royalty, Star's honesty could occasionally do with a little reining in. On the piste I could usually get the better of her, but in the music room she was madder than Bell End during the Nationals.

I left them to belt out some minor chords on their own while I sought solace in the pet shed, where Dorothy gave me some much-needed love and affection. I swear rabbits are ultra-sentient as far as creatures go, with little on their minds other than lettuce and carrots.

TWENTY

My Style Statement Depended on the Whims of a Psycho Toff

S ister Constance let Year Eleven off Saturday lessons so we could 'beautify ourselves for Operation Counter Dump,' which I must say was very Christian of her. She also let us order in pizza! The entire school almost fell over in shock. I know we do it all the time, but we do it secretly and smuggle in the delivery guy using the stealth and cunning that boarding school nurtures in teen minds.

Seriously though, getting dressed that day was more nerve-racking than getting dressed for my first social or VIP ball. My outfit had to be *ultra de rigueur*. When I say the pressure was on, I'm speaking euphemistically, you understand – or is that eurithmically? Either way, it was very stressful.

My outfit was largely inspired and owned by Honey.

For all her flaws, she does have her good points. Like Siddhartha, for example. We were all growing awfully fond of her orange-robed pacifist. Even Miss Bibsmore was developing a soft spot for him. Also, Honey did have an unreasonable number of designer outfits and shoes.

'Darling, you simply can't wear your own tragic clothes if you're serious about seducing poor Freddie,' my evil anti-girlfriend told me. 'I mean, they're probably the reason he dumped you, sweetie.' She was filing her talons as she explained this fact, adding, 'Besides, he has his pick of the crop, and well . . .' She let her sentence trail off, let the nail file fall to the floor and wiped an imagined tear from her eye. She always managed to make me feel that my life was too, too sad for mere words to express – and so she said it all with gestures. She's a perfectionist at miming my inadequacy.

Star et al agreed with her choice of coffee-coloured suede micro-mini. 'Oh yes, legs are always very now,' Georgina advised. The micro-mini was teamed with butter-coloured suede Jimmy Choos, which I feared would end in disaster. 'But what if I get them wet or dirty?' I asked fearfully. The last thing I wanted was to be hunted down by Honey and murdered for ruining her boots.

'Oh darling, they are soooo last term. It was you or the bin for them, to be perfectly honest.'

'Freds won't know that they're last season. Boys are hopeless on clothes,' Portia said kindly. 'Tarkie's got absolutely no idea about fashion, and Daddy's man sees to all his clothes.'

'I always think Tarquin looks really cool,' Indie said, which made us all tease her mercilessly about how feverishly infatuated she was with the ever-so-serious Lord Tarquin.

Star insisted I wear her ripped cashmere jumper. She said it would give me "attitude."

'The attitude of a girl with no boyfriend,' Honey remarked tartly. 'Well, if that's the look you're after, peasants, be my guest.' She sneered, lighting up a fag. Which provoked Star to pull out the Febreze and spray it all over my clothes and hair, making me choke. Seriously, my nerves were shredded by the time I'd been turned into boy bait.

Even though it was below zero, I wasn't allowed to wear tights 'because no one wants to pull a girl in granny tights,' as Georgina pointed out. 'Even Tobias can't bear them.' She grimaced as if the very thought of me in tights might be giving her a migraine.

Miss Bibsmore popped her head around the corner. 'She's right, duckie, you don't want to look like an old granny.'

'Oh well, you'd know, you horrible old hag,' Honey sniped.

Miss Bibsmore didn't rise to the bait. She merely shuffled off in her giant dog slippers. I think she knew that my style statement that day was in the hands of a psycho toff – and the last thing anyone wanted to do that day was set Honey off.

Georgina insisted on lending me one of her priceless pashes, which I'd been coveting since I first saw her wear it at the start of term. It was soooo gloriously soft and adorable, it reminded me of Dorothy until Honey wrapped it tightly around my neck like a hangman's noose.

Portia leant me her really beautiful diamond chandelier earrings, and Clems and Indie did my hair, which took an age because we wanted it to look wild and windswept and yet stay perfectly still. Indie had all sorts of lacquers and potions for that. Clems had a professional turbo hair dryer, which I was fairly certain started life as an aircraft engine.

I didn't wear any makeup whatsoever, apart from six inches of lip-gloss and three tubes of mascara, because everyone knows boys prefer the natural look.

My entire year was decked out in similar finery. Even the Polo twins looked like a Saint Tropez fantasy in tiny pleated skirts and gold strappy sandals. But it wasn't just them, everyone looked fantastic. Looking around at my beautiful posse as we began climbing into our taxis, I was struck by an overwhelming sense of pride. Bob's always banging on about the bonds of true friendship, but then he also bangs on about scrubbing vegetables, so I don't listen to him if I can help it. But for once, I really felt I understood what he meant – not about the veggie scrubbing, but about friendship and sisterhood. All these people were coming out for me, well, me and the school honour. I barely knew some of the girls, but they were there for me.

Braving the cold with their bare legs, all for the sake of my honour. It was a humbling experience.

Sister Constance and the rest of the nuns and all of the house spinsters were assembled in a long line on the gravel driveway to wave us off. Sister Regina and Sister Bethlehem had stitched a banner saying COUNTER DUMP YOUR SOCKS OFF GIRLS! which was très, très sweet and would have made me weep if my eyes weren't so weighed down with mascara. Miss Bibsmore saluted us with her stick. It almost brought a tear to my eye. Almost, because then I suddenly started to buckle under the monumental pressure of what I was about to do.

Fortunately, my *bête noir* took that moment to pinch me really hard on the arm and said, 'You look virtually pullable, darling.'

Actually we all looked ultra splendid. Everyone's heard that rumour about how Saint Augustine's girls have to take a test proving their beauty and a good figure rather than their intelligence to gain entry. I don't know if the rumours are true, but we really were stunning. And I say that with true humility and grace.

TWENTY-ONE

Lights-Camera-Action, Your Majesty

I had to hand it to Malcolm. He had pulled out all the stops for Operation Counter Dump. The film club, which I had imagined to be a small group of nerdy pale-skinned Goths, turned out to be gods freshly arrived from the heights of Mount Olympus.

I wasn't the only one gaping that day either. Over sixty wildly fit boys dressed in cool, ultra-anti-Sloane gear had assembled on the bridge in front of the castle town of Windsor. They looked, like, well, they looked like extras for a really well-lit independent film, actually. And they attracted a great deal of attention from locals and tourists alike.

Indie, Star, Georgina, Clems, Portia, Honey, Arabella, Fen, Perdita and – well, I won't go on listing them. But just picture forty-two Year Elevens, done up like catwalk models, climbing out of a fleet of taxis and minivans. And then picture those same girls coming face-to-face with the fittest boys Eades had to offer.

There was quite a kafuffle, I can tell you.

It was like a social without teachers. A capital VIP ball without bouncers – although personal security guards were everywhere, obviously. Siddhartha, in his flowing orange robes and revolving prayer wheel, stood apart from the other buzz cuts in their sharp suits and earpieces. I don't think the other security guys fully accepted him as one of their own. You could sort of sense their collective scorn for his monkish robes and peaceful demeanour.

As the boys came towards us like a tray of delicious walking sweets, tongues were lolling. That paragon of fitness, Lord Orlando Hunte, whom I'd met last Saturday, was using a video camera to film the two groups as they approached one another. We must have looked magnificently arty. It was one of those lights-camera-action moments that only comes around once in a lifetime – unless you're an It Girl or a Hollywood Star.

Malcolm was holding a megaphone, but sadly he didn't use it when he said, 'May I say, you look absolutely stunning this afternoon, Calypso?'

I didn't blush, but that was only because it was so cold and I couldn't feel my face. My heart did a little summersault, though. I was really touched, not just by his compliment, but by what he'd done for me. I mean, this whole dazzling show was all for me. And now that I knew he wasn't seeing Indie . . .

'Yes, Malcolm, you may tell me I look absolutely stunning this afternoon as long as I can thank you for, well, arranging all this,' I told him as I gestured at his posse.

'Desperate times call for desperate measures and all that,' he said grimly.

I wasn't quite sure what he meant by that, but I didn't get a chance to ask because he put the megaphone to his lips and shouted, 'I want to say on behalf of the Eades Film Society gathered here today that we are honoured to act as your decoys. Be assured, stunning creatures of Saint Augustine's, most of these gentlemen have dramatic experience of some sort, and everyone assembled here is one hundred percent on board with your, erm, Counter Dump situation. Isn't that right, gentlemen?' he asked his entourage.

I have to admit, I was finding him quite masterful and impressive. It didn't matter to me that most of the boys had ignored Malcolm's speech and continued chatting amongst themselves (apart from a few like Tarquin and Billy, who had wandered into the Saint Augustine's crowd to chat with girls they knew). On the other hand, the tourists and general public on the other hand, were openly gawking at this magnifique gathering.

Malcolm acted as if they'd all cheered him like the Romans cheered Mark Antony when he came to bury Caesar, not to praise him. I quite admired him for that.

'Right,' he said to the preoccupied crowd. 'So the plan is for Pyke elder to call Pyke younger and give him the signal to lead our quarry into the trap.'

I didn't like to interrupt his speech, but I tapped him on the shoulder. 'What quarry might that be?'

Malcolm looked confused. Then again, Malcolm always looked a little baffled. I think it's because his mind's always on a trillion things at once.

'Freddie,' Billy – otherwise known as Pyke elder – explained.

'Oh right, of course,' I said.

'You've got it.' I think Billy was finding the whole situation the apex of madness. 'So all set for Florence tomorrow?'

All this dumping and counter dumping had rather distracted me from my Big Dream, but I could hardly admit that to Billy, so I just nodded. Which is mad, because long before Freddie came into my life, all I thought about was being an international sabre champion. And now that the chance to make my mark was in my grasp, I was boy obsessing just as Star had warned.

Malcolm passed the megaphone to one of his entourage and asked Billy to make the call to Kev. He began to look around vaguely. Maybe he was searching for his director's chair.

Billy went over to the bridge so he could make the call to his brother in semi-privacy. When he came back, he gave Malcolm the nod. It was all very conspiratorial and exciting. I began to feel quite giddy.

Malcolm grabbed the megaphone back and told his film society, 'Right, gentlemen, this is it. You're having a jolly good time with this collection of stunningly fit girls. Just remember your roles. You're happy. You're relaxed. These are your salad days, chaps. Into character, move into the set, flirt with feeling and, action!'

With that, something miraculous happened. Suddenly, every boy was in animated conversation with the girls. I don't just mean the obvious suspects like Billy chatting to Portia, or Tarquin to Indie, but everyone seemed paired up even though there were about twenty more boys than girls. Though if you ask me, three to one is the perfect boy-girl ratio for any social situation. I even spotted Star flirting outrageously with Orlando. She was using that très obvious touching-the-buttons-of-his-shirt-as-she-spoke trick. Orlando looked bedazzled.

Next, Malcolm threw the full strength of his personality at me. He told me he'd fancied me from the moment he'd discovered me clinging to the wisteria vine outside his room like a wet rat. He told me that ever since that night he'd been distracted by thoughts of me. 'You see, the reason I kept on filing my DVDs and pretended not to take the least bit of notice of you was because I was terrified that I'd expose myself as an infatuated idiot. And that you'd despise me and think me pathetic.'

My jaw dropped for a bit as I tried to fathom whether he meant any of this stuff or was just acting 'in character.' All I could think of to say was, 'Oh fiddlesticks!' Honestly, I don't know where these hopeless blurtings come from.

'The plain truth of the matter, Calypso,' he said as he

brushed his hand across my jaw line and down my neck, which made me feel all wobbly and faint, 'is that I've never actually met anyone as funny or as diverse as you.'

'Gosh,' I blurted, staring up into his eyes. It was quite a change flirting with a boy who was miles taller than me. It does become quite tiresome flirting with the top of a boy's head – even if it does have really cool sticky-outy hair on it.

'You never cease to surprise me, Calypso. Sometimes after I've seen you or spoken to you, I have to hide in a cupboard and chortle myself sick.'

'Gosh!' I repeated. I can't remember all the things he said, but then I'm not such a loon that I actually believed him. I knew he was just trying to create the right dramatic effect. He was a director after all, and his role was to flirt. So in response to his speech to me, I rewarded him with one of my own flirtastic speeches.

'Oh Malcolm, I was mesmerised by you the moment I saw your head poke out of the window,' I told him as I twirled a tentacle of hair between my fingers. 'And I thought you were wildly sophisticated when you told me I could dry my wet clothes on your radiator. Actually, I was feverishly impressed that your radiator was warm; ours are only really there to give the idea of warmth. Oh, and also when you came to stay at the Clap House, I was ultra, ultra, ultra impressed by the way you dealt with those Gandalfs on the Landor Road. What was it, a Glasgow . . . ?'

'Kiss,' he said. It was probably my imagination, but he

seemed so close at that moment I thought I could feel his breath on my lips.

'That's it, *kiss*,' I agreed. 'Glasgow kiss.' And then for some unfathomable reason I did a Honey and batted my eyelashes and touched a button on his shirt. I suppose saying the word 'kiss' repeatedly to an older fit boy is enough to make any girl blush.

I was so giddy with my faux flirtarama, that I didn't notice Kev and Freds approach.

TWENTY-TWO

When Good Plans Go Bad

Freds was right by my shoulder when I finally felt his presence. I turned around and there he was. God he was soooo gorgeous. Soooo maddeningly fit, and he was standing so close I could smell that lovely lemony smell that was Freds. It was all I could do not to dribble.

'So what's all this, McHamish?' Freds asked cheerfully. He waved his arm at the gathered crew without even looking at me.

He was bloody smiling, in fact. He didn't look in the least bit heartbroken to see me – even in my stunning outfit! So I stared right into the centre of his soul. At least this forced him to notice me, but all he said was, 'How's it going, Calypso?'

I think 'flabbergasted' is the word – or is it 'flabberdashery'? Anyway, I was totally flabberdasheried, so I blurted, 'Fine, thank you very muchly,' in the most blankety blank way I could. I was still boring my eyes into his soul, but then he went and looked over my shoulder – quite a feat in itself given my height – and addressed Malcolm. It was as if I didn't even exist. 'Another film, McHamish, is it?' he asked.

Oh, this was brilliant. After all the effort my friends and I had put into my outfit. After all my careful non-application of makeup and Star's elaborate plans for The Counter Dump, not to mention her success at getting all these gods, I mean boys, together, this was how it was going to end. Freds was meant to realise what a fool he'd been to dump me, fall on his knees and beg me to take him back so I could dump him.

Instead, he appeared to be more interested in what a pack of boys he saw every day of the week was up to. I looked around at everyone. Couldn't he see they were all there for *moi*? For the sake of my dignity, in fact. But there was Freds, totally oblivious to all the organisation that had gone into creating the perfect circumstances for a Counter Dump.

It was a Waterloo if ever there was one. After all our careful strategising, Freds and Malcolm were going to have a nice little chat about the film society and my dignity would be forgotten. Talk about double Latin with knobs on.

That was when Malcolm kissed me. Not an air-kiss, or a peck on the cheek like your beardy aunt might give you after a few too many sherries. No, a proper snog-age. A proper grown-up, swoony woony, wobbly-kneed snog-age.

Ooh-la-la and va-va-va-voom! Malcolm knew a thing or two (or three, or four, or five) about this kissing business. He could run one of those kissing booths at county fairs when he grew up and positively rake in the cash. Though I don't suppose parents send their sons to the most prestigious boarding school in the world to have them setting up kissing booths.

It was such a mind-blowing kiss that even my brain stopped working. All I could do was feel and smell, and Malcolm felt and smelt lovely. Not like Freds, who always smelt of lemons. No, Malcolm smelt of boy, only in a nice way. If you could bottle Malcolm's smell you'd make trillions, I promise you.

I had the most alarming wobbly feeling in my tummy and disorientation of my little grey cells. I even started raising my left foot off the ground without any sort of cognitive instruction whatsoever.

And then he dipped me.

Yes, I swear, he dipped me! All I could think was ooh-la-la, this is just like in the movies. And then I remembered. This was a movie – well, sort of like a movie. Malcolm was playing the part of the gallant selfless hero making the idiot ex-boyfriend jealous.

Malcolm lifted me from the dip and I opened my eyes, which I hadn't even realised were closed. I knew boys liked you to close your eyes when they kissed you, but, well, I usually couldn't help looking at their scrunched-up little faces. Star says it's one of the few moments in life you get to see a boy vulnerable.

So anyway, I came to from my ooh-la-la moment and looked at Malcolm and realised for the first time how green his eyes were. Obviously, I already knew he had green eyes. A lot of these strawberry-blonde types with ivory skin are prone to green eyes. Malcolm's eyes were the colour of grass after the rain when all the positive (or is it negative?) ions are running rampant.

Then I looked around me like a blinking rabbit and saw everyone was staring at us. Everyone but Freds that is. He wasn't behind me anymore. Typical, I thought. I get dipped by an older fit boy, right under his stuck-up nose, and he wanders off. We couldn't afford to lose the evil prince at this delicate stage of The Counter Dump. So I asked the crowd at large, 'Where's Freds gone?'

Malcolm was still looking at me. He touched my chin and kissed me lightly on the lips.

'Where's who gone?' he asked.

'Freds!' I repeated. 'He's legged it.'

Malcolm looked around then as if coming to from a dream, but by that stage I'd already spotted Freds. He was only a few yards away, but there were lots of boys and girls between him and me, all flirting outrageously with one another, so he was sort of hidden from view. As I got a glimpse of his face, though, he looked distressed rather than bored. Also, he was sort of wobbling near the edge of the bridge.

For a moment it crossed my mind that maybe he *had* witnessed our snog-age after all and really was jealous and upset! And that made me feel even more confused.

Malcolm looked rather magnificent and powerful and superhero-ish as he moved towards Freds, especially when he shoved a few of the film society guys aside. I followed in his slipstream.

Malcolm cried out, 'He's not falling off the bridge, is he?'

The next thing I saw was my prince disappearing.

Then we all heard an almighty splash as he hit the Thames.

TWENTY-THREE

The Drowning Dreams of a Teenage Egoist

Malcolm yelled into his megaphone, 'Boy down!' and panic ensued as the security guys went loopity loopy loo. It was like a game of skittles gone wrong, the way they were all bumping into one another. Because a grave and terrible accident had befallen the heir to the throne, no one was laughing at their mad rush to get down the tiny cobbled steps with their enormous fat feet. But there was something vaudevillian about it all.

By the time they had descended one set of stairs, Freds had been washed to the other side of the bridge, so they had to rush in the other direction to mount their chaotic rescue mission.

It wasn't just Freddie's security on the case either. All of the other buzz cuts were falling over one another in their eagerness to rescue the drowning prince. You could hear their brains thinking, I swear! They were saying, 'Oh let me be the one to save His Majesty, please, Lord, let it be *me*!'

I say drowning because I'm prone to exaggeration, but actually, it must have been freezing in the Thames. The swans looked pretty chilly, and even outside the water, my legs were blue. I know people swim the Channel, but then they rub themselves with goose fat first, don't they? I was fairly sure Freds hadn't taken any such precaution.

The Eades Film Society and my own friends were all hanging off the bridge, yelling out, 'Freddie! Are you okay?'

As if anyone flailing about in a Thames swill in January could possibly be okay.

Just the same I joined them, dashing from one side of the bridge railings to the other as we watched our liege being helplessly washed downstream. Tourists were taking pictures of him. It was très, très tasteless and made me feel sick to the core. Sometimes I really have to question the morals of my fellow humans.

Eventually, I pushed my way through to the front of the crowd, spotted Freds and yelled out something not very useful to him like 'hang on!'

I don't think he heard me, though. He was focusing on trying to swim in subzero temperatures, against the current.

There was a woman on the bridge calling out to a gaggle – or is that a signature? – of swans. She's a bit of a Windsor fixture, actually. Mad as a pack of socks. She was wearing a big old grubby mac and bobble hat with earflaps, and as usual she was chucking chunks of bread to the swans.

So while the heir to the throne was drowning and the security guys were being pointless, the mad old woman continued to lob lumps of bread at her swans until one of the wretched bits hit poor Freds on the head.

Within a microsecond he was being mobbed by hundreds of frenzied swans. It was a horrifying sight! I'm normally quite fond of swans. I've spent many a happy moment watching the Windsor swans glide serenely down the Thames. But there was nothing serene about the way they were mobbing Freds. Seriously, they were all over him, wings and beaks lashing out in all directions in their feverish attempt to retrieve the lump of bread, which must have become wedged under Fred's collar.

He was utterly helpless to escape the ferocious force of flapping, hissing swans dragging their prince down into the depths of the current. I'm sure the irony wasn't lost on him either. It was just so wrong to see the monarch's own birds – which no one else is allowed to touch or eat apart from some odd college up at Oxford or something – attacking the future king.

'Leave him alone!' I screamed at the swans.

But would they listen? No. Daft birds. And the mad old woman was egging them on. 'Git him, my dearies! You git him! Trying to steal thee bread. You git him my dearies!'

Thee bread? Who talks like that? Proper loons, that's who.

The whole situation was just too dreadful. What if the tabloids got a shot of the swans trying to drown the prince? Everyone would say I was responsible. And they'd be right. If I hadn't attempted the stupid Counter Dump, Malcolm wouldn't have pulled me, and Freds wouldn't have fallen in the Thames and been flapped to death by ducks.

The prince's death would be on my hands.

I wouldn't be surprised if I was banished from England forever after this. Poor Bob and Sarah, imagining their beloved daughter happily floating on a blissful cloud of royal love, when actually I was a horrible prince killer.

Then I saw a flash of orange. It was Siddhartha diving into the Thames – and a truly magnificent sight it was. Seriously, he was like some wonderful orange-robed Olympian swimmer. What's more, he succeeded where the scrambling, bumbling, buzz cuts with their guns and wide boy attitudes had failed. He reached Freddie and bravely fought the swans off with his prayer wheel. He didn't hit them or anything unpeaceful like that, just sort of spun it around so it made a noise.

Anyway, taking the heir to the throne in one of his fin-like arms, he swam powerfully to the banks where the other security guys were eagerly waiting to take the glory. Oh yes, they threw their jackets over Freds and led him off to a fleet of waiting ambulances as if they'd been the heroes of the hour. The tabloid press was out in force by now, but I was too worried about Freds to bother death staring them. I tried to get through the crowd to the ambulance, but I was too late. Malcolm wrapped his own jacket around Siddhartha and led him off.

I just stood there alone, useless and embarrassed. 'Darling, are you all right?' Honey asked. 'Thank goodness my man had the presence of mind to rescue Freds or he might have died and you would have gone down for manslaughter, darling. You must feel terribly grateful and guilty.'

As numb as I was, I actually did feel grateful, and guilty. Honey was right. It was my fault.

'Darling, I couldn't bear to think of you languishing away in cold Old Chokey. Of course I'd send you care packages, although in my position you must realise our friendship could never continue. A girl of my social standing couldn't be seen associating with a con.'

'No, of course not,' I said, not really listening. Now was not the time to listen to psychobabble.

Star threw her arms around me and gave Honey a poke. 'Leg it, Honey, before I push *you* off the bridge,' she warned. 'Calypso didn't push Freddie in; he fell.'

Honey tried to raise her eyebrows but the Botox had paralyzed her brow so it just looked like her eyes were popping out of their sockets. 'Fine, I was just trying to be supportive.'

'Siddhartha was brilliant, though,' Star conceded. 'Malcolm's taken him back to Eades for a hot shower and a change of clothes.'

Honey went off on one. 'Well that's highly illegal. A security guard should never leave his or her principle.

Malcolm should have asked me before taking my man away.'

'The guy had just been dragged out of a freezing river, Honey,' Star pointed out. 'I think you should be grateful that someone had the semblance of mind to treat the hero of the hour.'

I could see it killed Honey to agree with Star, but after a short battle with herself she replied, 'Of course, I suppose under the circumstances I'll let it pass. He'd better dress him in orange, though. I don't want people mistaking him for a common security guard,' Honey warned. 'It's all been most distressing for me. Tell Siddhartha he can collect me at the pub. I'm going for a nice relaxing vod and ton. I'll see you back at the asylum, peasants,' she said, and flounced off.

Star put her arm around me. 'By the way, that was some kiss you had with Malcolm, darling!'

I knew she was just trying to lighten the mood and take my mind off Freds, but it only made me feel worse. And more confused, because it had been *some* kiss, even if it was just acting.

TWENTY-FOUR

A Severe Attack of the Mea Culpas

There were no girls lining the driveway to Saint Augustine's on our return. No banner-waving nuns skipping about triumphantly. No cheering house spinsters. Not even Misty – Miss Cribbe's incontinent spaniel – was there to lift a leg in salute. No, the drive was as empty as a desert. Bad news travels quickly in the royal county of Berkshire, I can tell you that much.

Operation Counter Dump had been a spectacular failure, and Saint Augustine's is feverishly keen to hush up spectacular failures. Instead of supportive, hopeful looks, *everyone* was giving me disappointed looks.

But other people's opinion wasn't my major concern. Freds was. I had to make sure he was okay. I needed to talk to him, to explain. But Eades had closed ranks like a rugby scrum or Fort Knox, or is that the CIA? The point is, they weren't leaking any news about the prince. Notice my use of the article, 'the' prince, not 'my' prince. He wasn't my prince anymore, and even though he was a wicked girl-dumping boy, I still cared for him. You don't just switch your feelings off for someone because they've dumped you by txt.

I spent the first part of the evening ringing/txting/e-mailing him to make sure he was okay. Then Star pointed out that his phone probably wasn't working if it was wet. I would have sent a carrier pigeon if I could have laid my hands on one. I even considered sending Dorothy. I mean, surely it would have melted the coldest heart to see little Dorothy hoppity hopping along with one of those little scrolls attached to her collar. Unfortunately, she has as much sense of direction (and intelligence) as a fig. Even amongst her fellow rabbits, she's known as the Queen of Daftness.

After all my energetic attempts at contacting Freds, I felt overcome by exhaustion and threw myself on my bed like Ophelia in that painting by Millais. Okay, so Ophelia threw herself in some reeds, but where was I supposed to find reeds at that time of night? I couldn't even bring myself to go down to supper to face the buggery grey slops even if it did mean being marked down as a suspected anorexic. Nothing seemed to matter now. I was in the grip of a powerful bout of ennui.

Star tried to drag me out of my ennui (also known as my pillow), but I shunned her.

'Come on, darling, you have to eat,' she pleaded, pulling at my limp body. You're flying to Florence tomorrow, and you'll need the energy to rinse the Italians.'

'Bring back something in your pocket for me,' I told her, punching my pillow in a vain attempt to make it more comfortable. Sarah hasn't bought me a new pillow since Year Seven, which means it is now as hard and thin as cardboard. 'Anyway, I don't want to go to Florence.'

'Don't be daft, all this will be forgotten once you get to Italy, and I can't bring back mash and chops in my pocket. Besides, I'm so ravenous I'll probably woof down everything I can get my lips around.'

'Oh well, if you can eat with a half-drowned boy on your conscience, don't let me stop you,' I told her.

'Darling, I am sure he's fine. If you're really worried, ring Malcolm and find out what's going on.'

'Ring Malcolm?' I shrieked, pulling my face out of my pillow. 'Are you mad? I can't ring Malcolm after our circus of snog-age! Can't you see, my nutty little friend, I'm the reason Freds fell in the Thames and almost drowned.'

'No, you're not. It was a loose cobble, that's all. Could have happened to anyone.'

'A loose cobble?' I repeated, remembering how careful you have to be, especially at the end of the bridge heading to Windsor Castle. There was a large gap in the railing at the end where people tether their bikes and the cobbles slip down into the Thames.

'Yes, a loose cobble. I told you it wasn't your fault. Now stop being morbid and come down to supper.'

I was in a dense and confusing soup of emotions. I mean, of course I didn't like feeling guilty, but at least guilt made me feel central to the tragedy. 'So, he *wasn't* overcome by jealousy?'

Star shrugged.

I sighed. 'Well, cobble or no cobble, he still fell in the Thames because of our stupid attempt at honour saving. Admit it, the entire Counter Dump plan was an exercise in madness from start to finish.'

Star tutted.

'It's true. I mean Freds has practically grown up in Windsor Castle and he's never fallen in the Thames before, has he?' With that, I pressed my face into my cardboard pillow again, striking a moving pose of *mea culpa* if ever there was one. Although I wasn't certain how long I could keep it up. It's not easy to breathe through cardboard.

'Well, I hate to say I told you so, but I did tell you to dump Freds at the start of term. If only you'd listened to me, none of this would have happened.' Before I could reply Star flounced out of my room. Only then she came back and asked, 'So, what was it like? Kissing Malcolm, I mean.'

I threw a purple cushion at her.

There was no way I was calling Malcolm. I was never going to think of him or speak to him again. In fact, I would never so much as look at him. If I passed him on the streets of Windsor, I resolved to avert my eyes and pretend to be absorbed in something else.

Unfortunately, my subconscious refused to cooperate.

Once Star was off to feed from the refractory slops trough, I fell asleep and dreamed of kissing Malcolm again. It was très, très distressing, especially when I woke up and discovered I had two missed calls from him – but he hadn't left a message. Typical boys.

When the others came back from supper, they were really sweet. Indie, Clems, Arabella, Portia, Star and even Honey had all smuggled something back for me. Unfortunately, it was covered in pocket lint, so it wasn't all that appetising, but I was grateful for the thought.

Everyone tried to chivvy me out of my attack of the *mea culpaisms*, apart from Honey, who kept shaking her head and saying things like, 'You must feel awfully responsible, darling.'

But everyone ignored Honey.

Portia reminded me that we were flying to Italy the next day for our first outing with the national team. Poor naive child, she probably thought that a trip to Italy was all it would take to lift my spirits.

'I won't be able to go now,' I told her sorrowfully.

'Darling, I know you feel bad about the way things worked out today, but you have to put it from your mind now. Apart from anything else, you have an obligation to the team.'

I lifted my face millimetres from the pillow and inhaled some air. Then I said, 'I honestly can't see how I'll be much use to the team when I'm paralysed with shame and misery.' Then I pushed my face back into my pillow of shame to demonstrate my point.

Georgina held the face of Tobias up to me so that his nose was rubbing against my cheek. 'Darling, please pull yourself together. You know Tobias can't bear defeatist attitudes, and no one will remember the failed Counter Dump if you come back with a cup.'

'And Bell End will run you through with his sabre if you don't regain your focus,' Portia pointed out. 'And there's the rest of the team to consider, not to mention your nemesis, Jenny Frogmorten. What will toilet-mouth Jenny say? She'll say you're a chicken and make mad clucking sounds. You can't give her the satisfaction. Come on, darling, let's pack.'

The thought of Jenny galvanised me into immediate action. Portia was right, *mea culpa* or no *mea culpa*, I wasn't going to have Jenny Frogmorten make clucking noises about me.

After we packed, we unpacked.

And then we packed and unpacked and packed some more because The Rules dictated that we were only allowed one piece of hand luggage for our three-night stay in the Style Central Paradise of Italy. Oh, the bally merdeness of it all.

'How can a girl be expected to squeeze hair dryers, straightening tongs, makeup bag and a don't-I-look-effortlessly-fabulous wardrobe into one piece of hand luggage? It defies the laws of physics and nature!' I said.

Portia was as frantic and frustrated as me. We were putting things in and taking them out all night long. Now I knew how Sisyphus felt, rolling his wretched stone up and down the hill night and day.

Still, at least it took my mind off my shame . . . and kissing Malcolm. I checked my mobile one more time before entrusting it to Indie. It was a wrench being parted from my mobile, I can tell you. But as it didn't have roaming, I wouldn't have a signal in Italy anyway.

TWENTY-FIVE

Sic Transit Gloria Mundi

By all accounts, the battle in the convent over who would act as our chaperones was bitterly fought. Sister Regina and Sister Bethlehem were the elected winners. The rancour amongst the other nuns was palpable when we knocked on the door the next morning. I suspected Sister Regina of rigging the Hail Mary competition, or whatever other mad nun method they used to decide the vote.

Heaven knows how Sister Bethlehem landed herself a trip to Italy, though. I mean, I don't want to be disrespectful about old nuns or anything, but she is over one hundred years old and rapidly slipping into her peaceful end via sleep. If she'd been awake for more than an hour in any one day in the past decade, I'd eat my knickers.

Bell End had to carry her to the van.

And he dropped her.

But not even that woke her up.

The other chaperone was Sister Regina, who had done us proud at the Nationals. I was quite pleased to see her little four-foot frame sitting proudly alongside Bell End on her cushion in the van. She tooted the horn she was so excited, which woke up Sister Bethlehem, who rambled off a decade of the rosary before falling back into a deep sleep. How these two nuns were going to protect us from bottom-pinching Italians was anyone's guess.

As we drove towards Gatwick, I couldn't help reflecting on last term's trips to tournaments when Sarah had accompanied us. Now all I warranted was a last-minute phone call. I suppose she was too busy snog-aging Bob these days to bother with my fencing competitions. Actually, on second thought, it was better they didn't come to Italy. Those two certainly didn't need to fan the flames of their romance in Florence, one of the world's most romantic cities.

The plan was that Portia, Bell End, the nuns and I would meet the rest of the national team at Gatwick, three hours before the flight. Yes, you heard correctly, three hours!

'Why three hours?' I asked, because to be honest, I could have used the extra sleep. Clems' snoring was not improving despite the rather stylish nose clip Indie and I had manufactured for her out of duct tape and hair clips.

'To avoid delays, Kelly. Put your brain into gear, girl,' Bell End turned around and yelled at me. Seriously, he was so wound up, the veins in his neck were throbbing. He was stressed enough at the national tournaments last term, and I began to fear what was he going to be like at our first international tournament.

At the airport, people were yelling, children were weeping and one horrible man in flip-flops – yes flip-flops – told our little Sister Regina to 'bugger off' when she asked for directions to the check-in counter.

Sister Regina was ever so sweet about it too. All she said was, 'God bless you, my son.'

I felt like slapping him about the face with one of his snotty little flip-flops, but Sister Bethlehem stomped on his foot with her wooden clogs. For a woman who passed her first century last year, she has a lot of fight left in her – when she's not asleep, that is.

Bell End had been off at the loo during our encounter with flip-flop man, but when I told him about the incident, he became enraged. 'I'd have run the blighter through with my sword, had I been here.' Then he looked at me as if I should have meted out a similar punishment. 'Well, Sisters, I shan't leave your side again. While blaggards like that crawl the earth, decent men must be on their guard.'

Portia and I were quite pleased when Billy found us. After we'd dispensed with the requisite air-kisses, it didn't escape my eagle eye that a certain longing look passed between Billy and Portia. Even in this barren hall of airline chaos, love would have its way.

'How's Freds?' I asked him after their longing gaze had become très embarrassing.

'Not too well,' he told me, turning his deep blue eyes onto me. 'He spent the night in the infirmary, apparently.'

'I feel really bad,' I told him, hoping that he'd say something reassuring like, 'Don't blame yourself, Calypso. Why, chaps like Freds fall in the Thames all the time.' But all he did was nod and go back to gazing longingly at Portia.

A bit later, we spotted Jenny and a few other members of the national team lurking outside a bookstore. Jenny gave me a death glare. After everything that had happened at the Nationals, I was resigned to having Jenny as my anti-girlfriend. I was far from scared, however. Mostly because I doubted her ability to out-psycho Honey. Not to boast, but years of being blanked by girls at Saint Augustine's had given me a profound ability to out–death stare the best of them.

Bell End dived on a tall gentlemen in a cravat. The guy looked like he'd just swallowed his own bottom when he clapped eyes on our mad master.

'Ah, Commodore!' Bell End cried, shaking the man's hand vigorously. 'How the devil are you, mate?' Then he slapped the poor fellow hard across the arse. I think Bell End was aiming for the guy's back but missed. The Commodore was very tall compared to Bell End.

But Bell End laughed like there was no tomorrow.

'Girls, meet The Commodore, the head of the GBR national team. He and I were warriors once. *Mano a mano* and all that.' He then gave a little bow and – I am not lying

– clicked his heals together. It was all rather tragic and tear jerking. I know it's disloyal, but sometimes I wish Bell End had a bit more élan like our last fencing master, Professor Sullivan.

The Commodore didn't look pleased to see his old comrade. 'Yes, well, that was all a very long time ago.'

Bell End winked at Portia and me. It was très, très mortifying. 'Many a time I gave The Commodore here a good thrashing, eh?'

Comparing the implausibly tall form of The Commodore and the short, stocky build of our master, I somehow doubted it.

I think Bell End sensed a collective dubiousness amongst the crowd because he continued. 'Bigger the target, the more you've got to work with, see.' Then, he started leaping and darting about The Commodore, using his finger as an imaginary sabre to jab him.

It was beyond mortifying.

'I'm sure you distinguished yourself admirably, Mr Wellend,' Sister Regina said, her little arms folded neatly inside the sleeves of her habit.

I could tell Sister Regina wasn't impressed by The Commodore. Years of convent living had bred in her an innate distrust of men. Bell End was one thing – apart from anything else he was very kind and gallant with her. But I could tell she definitely considered this chap in the cravat a stuck-up fool of the highest order.

I was inclined to agree with her on the basis that the guy

was wearing trousers that barely reached his ankles, and don't even get me started on the cravat. I gave him a little bow just the same, which sent Portia off into a fit of chortles. Sister Bethlehem had fallen asleep on my hand luggage by this stage, so we agreed to leave her there until the rest of the team arrived.

Portia and I sat on her hand luggage and practiced the élan, panache, vitesse, finesse and va-va-voom we'd need if we were to cope with the sophisticated rigours of Italy. Come to think of it, all those qualities were French, though I'm sure the Italians have the same qualities and more. It's no secret that the Italians rule the world in matters of *amore* and *la dolce vita*, which I think means beautiful life, or nice biscuits – one or the other. Also, Italy gave us Michelangelo's *David*, the fittest statue ever chiselled. I think His Marbleness might even be in Florence, actually.

'We must visit *David* while we're in Florence,' I remarked to Portia, as she sat glamorously on her hand luggage, flicking through *Italian Vogue*. How anyone could look glamorous on the floor of an airport, I'll never know. I suppose the *Italian Vogue* helped. The centuries of breeding didn't hurt either.

'Yaah, deffo,' she agreed, turning another page. 'And lots of lovely leather shops,' she added. 'The moment we arrive we shall hit the Ponte Vecchio. *Pronte!*'

That was another thing; Portia spoke Italian. Not surprising really, given she did and knew everything that is deemed to be sophisticated. No wonder Freds had dumped me. I was about as sophisticated as Disneyland. 'I think the only word I know in Italian is *amore*,' I told Portia dismally. 'And the only boy I've ever *amore*-ed, dumped me.'

'*Pazzo*,' Portia said.

I wasn't sure *pazzo* sounded very *simpatico*, so I added, 'Oh, and I know *simpatico*, *molto*, *grazie*, *prego*, *bella*, *avanti* and *mal*.'

'So practically fluent,' Portia remarked.

'*Molto fluento*,' I agreed as I fanned myself with my ticket at the shock of discovering I knew an entire language I'd never even studied. 'Sister Constance is right. The teenage brain truly is remarkably absorbent.'

'Still, you'd best absorb *pazzo* while you're at it darling,' Portia insisted.

'*Pazzo*?'

'It means "bonkers,"' she explained.

I wasn't quite sure what she meant by that remark, but I didn't want to go there. 'Do you think we should start smoking?' I asked. 'I mean, all Italians smoke, don't they? We don't want to appear feverishly unworldly in front of all those fit Italian fencing boys.'

Portia shook her head. 'I'm not smoking. We're not going to choke our lungs when we're going to Italy to represent our country in a sporting event.'

I almost fainted when she said that – the representing 'our' country bit, I mean.

As I looked around at our entourage, it started to really

sink in. We were going to Florence to represent *our* country. I know I'm American. I mean, I was born there. I grew up on cheeseburgers and Cokes just like millions of other American teens with *pazzo* 'rentals. But as I was going to school in England, I could hardly be much use to the American fencing team, could I? But maybe, just maybe, if I did really, really feverishly well, one day I *would* fence for my real country. My secret dream – the dream of me fencing for the US in the Olympics – suddenly seemed closer.

I was distracted in my wild imaginings by Jenny, who had embarked on a pathetic attempt at chatting up Billy. I wondered briefly if Portia was jealous, but I suppose she noticed, as I did, that he didn't take his adoring gaze off Portia for a moment.

The rest of the team arrived in dribs and drabs. There were eighteen fencers on the team altogether; three girls and three boys on the foil, épée and sabre teams, respectively. It didn't escape Jenny's notice that Portia and I were the only team members with an entourage.

'God, you're such babies, needing a teacher and nuns to look after you,' she scorned. 'My parents let me do everything on my own,' she boasted.

I was rather disappointed in her standard of poisonous put-downs. Jenny had a long way to go before she could challenge Honey for the crown of Torture Queen.

The schools and families of the other team members clearly trusted their charges to The Commodore, which struck me as *molto* irresponsible. In addition to Bell End and the nuns, we also had a physiotherapist – a man of rather extraordinary physical proportions. Mind you, he'd be more likely to trip over a muscle than be of any use in a skirmish.

Bell End had introduced him earlier as Dr Draculochovichidoo or some mad name like that and then went on to explain that Dr Draculochovichidoo was there to tend to muscular aches and injuries.

'To keep your body oiled and fully operational' was how he actually put it.

Utterly *pazzo*.

Gatwick was experiencing delays that day. Big surprise there. We finally boarded the flight nine hours later. Yes, nine. I counted off the passing of each torturously boring hour out loud, hoping to teach Bell End a lesson about arriving too early for flights. But he pretended to ignore me.

Portia was seated between Billy and another really fit boy on the sabre team who had every jaw on the Alitalia plane scraping the floor in awe. Some heiresses get all the luck.

Bell End sat beside The Commodore. The physio guy was in front with a couple of pimply foilists. His name being unpronounceable, we decided to call him Fizz Whiz. When I say *we*, I mean Sister Regina and Sister Bethlehem, who were seated on either side of me. Sister Bethlehem was out like a light before they started showing us how to put our seat belts on and jump off the inflatable shoots. Sister Regina proved a chatty and lively companion, especially after the drinks trolley had been around a few times.

'Sister, you can't keep stealing all those brandies,' I scolded my little bearded nun as she pocketed another handful when the flight attendant wasn't looking.

'They're for Sister Bethlehem,' she explained sweetly when the flight attendant turned around and caught her red-handed. The flight attendant must have fallen for her charms because she said '*va bene*,' handed Sister another bundle of brandies and winked.

By the time we disembarked at Pisa airport, Sister had pocketed about five dozen brandy miniatures. Mind you, I think Bell End had drunk about the same amount on the flight. He wove around customs like a shopping trolley with a dodgy wheel, boasting about his Olympic medal, flashing it to the customs officials and anyone else we passed. The Italians showed a congenial aloofness, which I admired.

Because there were so many of us, we needed a coach to take us all to our pensione in Florence. I was too tired to take much in, but from the little I saw from the coach window, Florence was the very apex of *bellissima*. Everything looked so postcard historic, and as for the Italians, well, they were everywhere; smoking their heads off and sipping espresso just as I had always imagined.

'I think you might be wrong about the smoking thing,' I told Portia. 'They're all at it.'

But she assured me she was right. 'I bet they're tourists anyway,' she told me with enormous authority. 'Probably French.' Then she curled her upper lip in distain.

The Pensione Bella was down a cobbled lane that was far too narrow for the coach, so we had to lug our kit for something like, oh, five thousand yards. I finally saw the sense in the hand luggage rule.

Pensione Bella was lovely. It was *bella*, in fact. It was run by a little old lady about the same height as Sister Regina who refused to speak to anyone other than our little nun. And it wasn't because no one else spoke Italian either. She snubbed Portia like she was of lowly peasant stock and sneered at my feverishly convincing Italian-accented English. Also, she kept using words that began with 'mal,' which I know from my Latin classes means 'evil.'

Bell End and the Signora had a bit of a battle over the luggage-carrying business, but Signora Santospirito physically beat him off. Hitting him over the head, she shouted, *'Tchuk! Tchuk! Malfagio, tchuk!'* Which I can only imagine was très, très unkind. Poor Bell End.

He valiantly attempted to regain his gallantry by carrying Sister Bethlehem in a fireman's lift up the stairs. But as she slept through the entire exhausting haul, it was a thankless task. Jenny made a sneering remark about him, which made me feel even more protective of our mad old master.

We'd agreed to convene in the courtyard in half an hour, or as The Commodore put it – twenty-three-hundred hours sharp, whatever that meant. Despite how exhausted and grotty we all felt, and the lateness of the hour, The Commodore was most insistent that we go over our strategies for the fencing pools tomorrow. The sensible suggestion offered up by Billy that we chat about it over breakfast the next day was spurned. Apparently, The Commodore liked *total* silence at breakfast.

When the Signora finally deigned to hand over the key to our funny little attic room, Portia and I were left with Jenny as our roommate. A feverish *déja vu* feeling of sharing with Honey last term washed over me.

Our scheduled meeting only gave Portia, Jenny and me ten minutes in which to fight over who could use the bathroom. Portia and I decided with a shared look to let Jenny win. At Saint Augustine's we knew the importance of avoiding the small battles and saving your muscle for the big ones. I think Jenny was peeved that we'd caved so easily.

To freshen up, Portia and I squirted one another with Evian. Then we changed into something more stylishly *belle*. Also, while Jenny was taking a bath, we enjoyed our view of the sepia-and-burnt-umber-tinted city with its narrow lanes, arched bridges and domed roofs. Portia tried to teach me a bit more vital Italian, but I assured her that I'd get by with my gift for accents.

From where we stood on the funny old metal beds with their lovely white damask spreads, we could see the Ponte Vecchio arched over the Arno River. It looked most *tranquillo*, which according to Portia means . . . tranquil.

A last look in our aged-speckled mirror revealed that while Portia oozed style from every aristocratic pore of her being, Jenny and I would have to make do with lashings of lip-gloss and mascara. I thought I sensed a slight thawing in Jenny as I offered her my lip-gloss. Everyone knows lip-gloss is the international symbol of friendship for girls everywhere. But then she dashed my hopes by saying, 'You'd better not have herpes, Kelly.'

She still used it, though.

Then I began to worry that *she* might have herpes, but I didn't say anything. I had to save my energy for the big battles.

TWENTY-SIX

The Insubordination of The Commodore

The meeting was held in the lovely downstairs courtyard. It was a large open tiled area lit by tea-lights. In the centre, there was a marble fountain with a cherub peeing in its own little puddle. The atmosphere was most un-*tranquillo*, though.

I had imagined we were convening to get to know one another. We'd all been introduced at the airport, but I had forgotten almost everyone's names because we'd peeled off into our own little groups pretty much straightaway.

Eventually, The Commodore stood up, which was daunting in itself given his height, and then he coughed. I moved my chair away a bit in case he had a germ – I mean, I didn't want to be sick for my first international tournament.

'Right, well, everyone seems to be present and correct,' he began – whatever that meant. 'Welcome to, erm, Florence. I hope you have all settled in. The tournament will kick off with the pools at eleven hundred hours tomorrow. I propose we go on patrol at o-six hundred hours.'

'What do you mean by "on patrol," exactly?' I asked anxiously. I am not a girl born to patrol at o-six hundred hours or any other hour for that matter.

'I agree,' Billy added. 'If we're not going to the salle until eleven, why do we have to go on patrol at six?'

The Commodore pointed at Billy, which according to Sister Constance is the vilest thing you can do to another human being. Then again, Sister Constance has led a very sheltered life in the convent and doesn't watch cable television. 'I'll warn you now, Pyke, I won't tolerate insubordination in my ranks.'

'Oh, sod off then,' Sister Regina told him, which turned the courtyard into a gigglerama that even had Signora Santospirito joining in. That was how The Commodore's authority began its downward slide. I sensed it would be a festival of insubordination from that point on.

I also confirmed that Sister Regina had already been tucking into her brandy stash when she brazenly pulled a few miniature bottles from her sleeve and poured them into glasses, which were miraculously produced by the Signora. She passed the miniatures to Sister Bethlehem, Bell End, Fizz Whizz and the Signora – significantly, there was no glass set down for The Commodore. I noticed a vein in The Commodore's neck throbbing violently, but he didn't say anything.

Bell End gallantly held up his glass to the Signora in a toast, and Signora's eyes twinkled. She nodded approvingly and smiled. Bell End had a way with the prickliest ladies, that was for sure.

Even though everyone started complaining about how exhausted they were, Sister Regina insisted we explore the nightlife. 'Let's go and have a jig at one of those discothèque thingamees I read about in the travel guide to Florence,' she suggested, nudging Sister Bethlehem to back her up. Sister Bethlehem took a sip of her brandy and smiled serenely. 'Come on, we don't get out much. Don't be such sticks-in-the-mud,' she urged. 'Take pity on us poor nuns and take us out for a jig.'

'But we're underage,' Portia said.

Sister Regina tutted. 'Nonsense child! This is Italy; they don't worry about details like age. Besides, I won't tolerate ageism. We take a very dim view of that at the convent, I can tell you.'

Nuns really are in a special little *pazzo* world. And Bell End was no saner. He fully backed Sister up.

'Champion idea,' he agreed, nudging The Commodore in the ribs. 'What do you say, Commodore, eh? Let's get our dancing shoes on. Show these young ones a few steps on the dance floor, shall we? Eh? Eh? What do you say, Commodore?'

By this stage The Commodore's neck vein looked on the verge of bursting. He spoke to Bell End through gritted teeth. 'My name is Mr Rogers, as you well know,

Oscar. But I'm happy for you to call me Biffy if you'd prefer.'

I know, how sad and funny to know your teacher's first name!

'Can we call you Biffy too, sir?' I blurted, which sent Portia, Jenny and the rest of the team into fits of giggle-dom. One of the other guys, an épéeist, I think, even stood up and shook my hand.

Biffy didn't respond to my request, but he agreed with Sister and Bell End that a 'bit of light entertainment' might help the team unwind and bond. I suspect he was trying to claw back some authority.

So Bell End, Biffy, the nuns, Fizz Whiz, Portia, Jenny, Billy, myself and the rest of the team (whose names I still didn't know) set off into the late Tuscan evening for a jig. Signora Santospirito had apparently given Sister the skinny on the happening place to go and get down.

'Are you a betting man, Mr Biffy?' Sister Bethlehem asked as we wandered through the cobbled lanes.

'I like the occasional game of bridge, and I take a flutter at Ascot if I have a good tip.'

'What about ten quid on who cut Samson's hair?' she asked Biffy, looking at him with her fluffy little innocent nun face.

Nuns. There's no stopping them.

TWENTY-SEVEN

Discothèque Pazzo

I presumed the discothèque would be full of chubby old mustachioed Italian men in gold chains. I envisioned them swinging their wives around the dance floor to Tony Bennett songs while a tattered old disco ball lolled from the ceiling.

Instead, Cavern was a dark, lively, thumping, strobe-lit extravaganza of hip-hoppity music. The doormen didn't look twice at our *pazzo* crowd of nuns, fencing masters and underage teens. He said something to us in Italian, and I worshipped Portia when she replied.

There was the odd mustachioed man decked out in gold chains on the dance floor, but he was the exception. Mostly the club was packed with fit boys and stunning girls in ooh-la-la outfits, smoking cigarettes and sipping sophisticated drinks.

Billy and the other guys asked the girls what we wanted to drink. Sister Regina asked for two limoncellos for her and the now feverishly excited Sister Bethlehem. I swear she was tapping her little wooden hobnailed shoes to the beat. Most of us went for soft drinks, but Jenny had to show off by asking for an elaborate cocktail. Before we'd left the pensione, I'd clocked her stuffing knickers in her bra. I dreaded where this evening would end if Jenny got drunk and pulled.

I thought Biffy might object to the cocktail but he nodded agreeably and wrote down all our orders on a little pad he produced from his jacket of many pockets. Then he went off to the bar with the boys. He was soooo obviously sucking up.

'Let's check out the loos,' Jenny suggested, a proposal that met with solid approval from her friends. 'I heard they have those squat jobbies in Italy,' she announced, as if this prospect thrilled her. If you want my opinion, I think she'd noticed what the rest of us had already discovered: one of her knickers was peeping out of her top.

'I'll stay here and try to grab a table,' I told them.

There would be time enough for squat toilets later. Right now, someone had to be sensible, and it wasn't going to be Bell End, Biffy or the nuns, that was for sure.

'Oooh, isn't this fun, Mr Wellend? I do hope you'll be putting your name on my dance card,' Sister Regina told him as I looked about for a table. Sister Bethlehem looked as awake as the next person, but I figured that was unlikely to last. When she popped off she'd need a chair at the ready.

'If it isn't Calypso, she who drags men from their duties,' a voice behind me said.

I turned and there he was. Malcolm McHamish's Italian doppelganger. He had an unlit cigarette stuck to his lower lip and a glass of something in his hand. I looked him up and I looked him down and then I looked him up and down again. He was wearing a pair of sunglasses perched on his head, an Italian suit over an open-necked Pucci shirt, but apart from his continental taste in clothes, he was a Malcolm clone. Then my little grey cells got to work and I wondered how this stranger knew my name.

I swear if I hadn't been so shocked I would have fainted. It really was Malcolm!

'As ever, you look the very epitome of style and beauty, Miss Kelly,' he said. 'Did you just get here? It's the damndest thing, don't you know. I've been ringing and ringing you for days. Well, that is to say all day.' A waiter passed by and lit the cigarette dangling from Malcolm's lips. Malcolm thanked him profusely in Italian and gave him a wad of Euros.

'What are you doing here? How's Freddie?' I asked in a rush.

Malcolm took a deep drag on his fag before continuing. 'Ah, you want the latest goss on His Royal Nibs. Sick as a cat, poor devil. Spent the night in the infirmary, which is enough to kill off the best of them.'

'Is he going to be okay?' I asked anxiously. 'I mean, I've tried to call him. I feel awful about what happened.'

Malcolm put his hand on my arm and gave me a comforting rub. 'Why? You've not been tinkering with the cobbles at the edge of the bridge, have you? No, darling Freds is made of tougher stuff than that. They sent him home this morning while the antibiotics work their magic.' I watched as Malcolm exhaled his smoke and blew a series of rings that wafted up to the ceiling. It was probably my feverish imagination, but he seemed bored by the conversation somehow. Which made me want to tap-dance for his attention.

'What are *you* doing here, in Italy, though?' I asked.

He waved his fag around. 'Oh, you know, the usual. Immersing myself in the trough of Florence nightlife. Here, try this Disaronno, I swear it tastes like marzipan. Reminds me of Christmas,' he urged, shoving his glass to my lips.

I took a sip and grimaced. 'Yes, marzipan,' I agreed, pushing the glass away. 'But why aren't you at Eades?'

'Oh that. Yes, well, bit of a last-minute thing. The Film Society took a vote and the ayes had it, I'm afraid.'

'A vote on what?'

'Filming the British team fencing in Florence. Also we thought we might get a bit of that heady Renaissance air into our lungs, touch up our Italian language skills and buy a few trinkets for the old madres back home.'

I shook my head, still convinced he was a mirage. Then I caught Bell End swinging the nuns around the dance floor and knew that all was as it should be in my mad little world.

'Sorry, I seem to be banging on about me,' he said, taking hold of my hand. 'Come and join us for a drink.'

I allowed myself to be led over to where it seemed half the Eades Film Society were sprawled out in a large roped-off VIP booth. All of them were dressed like they'd just come from a magazine shoot for Prada or Versace. They barely acknowledged me until Malcolm chucked an ice cube at Orlando.

'You all know Calypso, the Botticelli angel of Saint Augustine's,' Malcolm announced.

They all smiled or raised their drinks, and then it took about a five full minutes to air-kiss them all. Even then, most of them continued chatting to one another as they brushed my cheeks with their lips. 'Ah, and there is the beautiful Portia,' Malcolm cried out as I was still air-kissing the troupes. He waved to her, and she peeled off from the rest of the fencing group and came over.

Another round of air-kissing commenced. Then Malcolm asked, 'What would you like to drink, Portia? I recommend the Disaronno.'

'I've ordered, thanks, Malcolm. Billy's here with us, you know. What are you doing here?' This last question was directed at Tarquin, but he just held his drink up in a toast and carried on an animated discussion with Orlando.

Malcolm replied. 'Yaah, likes his sabre does our Pyke. No, he's one of the heroes that drew us here. Rather hoping to get some triumphant footage of the boy wonder making mincemeat of the legendary Italian swashbucklers.' Then he turned his attentions back to me. 'Calypso, you'll be wanting your usual.' He shouted out to Orlando,

'Hunte, get a bottle of Veuve, will you? Get two, in fact, three, four – a dozen! In fact, tell them to empty the bar.' Then he flung down a huge pile of Euros on the table.

'Get it yourself, McHamish,' Orlando replied, lazily chucking the notes back at Malcolm. 'I went last time.'

'Honestly, I don't want any champagne,' I told Malcolm.

'Nonsense, you live on the stuff.'

'No, I don't,' I told him truthfully.

'Really?' Malcolm looked shocked. 'Well, why are you always swilling the stuff down, then?'

'I'm not always swilling the stuff,' I said with lashings of indignance. 'I don't even like the taste of it.'

Malcolm wiped a stray lock of his slicked-down hair from his face. 'Excuse me, Calypso, but you are a champagne swiller of the highest order. The first night I met you hanging off the wisteria vine outside my room – vision of loveliness though you were – I thought, Malcolm this is not your usual girl. McHamish, old chap, this is a girl who lives life on the edge. Pissing down with rain it was, long after midnight, and yet there you were climbing vines looking for boys. No stopping this one, I said to myself. And then you accepted my invitation to dry off in my room, draped your lingerie on my radiator and made a beeline for the champagne fridge.'

'I was lost,' I explained, outraged. 'I was looking for Freddie, remember? And you offered me the champagne.'

'Ah, but you knocked it back like it was your mother's own milk, as I recall.'

Portia pulled herself away from her brother Tarquin to say, 'She only drank it because she was trying to be polite. Calypso barely ever drinks.'

Malcolm rolled his eyes and then held up his hand to halt further discussion. 'Campari and soda, it is then,' he announced, disappearing into the throng before I could explain that I couldn't drink on the night before the tournament.

TWENTY-EIGHT

Developing My Aptitude in Matters of La Dolce Vita

The Campari and soda was red. Not that I could drink it, but it contrasted nicely with my green dress, so I swirled it around with my straw, hoping it would make me appear fabulous. Even though I wasn't smoking, I was fairly confident that I looked *molto, molto* sophisticated swirling my elegant drink about with my swizzle stick while all around me *pazzo* reigned supreme.

Sister Bethlehem had obviously been storing up reserves of energy during all her years of napping because she didn't leave the dance floor all night. In fact, Bell End, Sister Regina, Biffy and Fizz Whiz were all tripping the light fantastic.

Malcolm, Billy, Tarquin, Orlando et al. did some fancy dancing too.

'There's no way they'd dance like that in England,'

Portia remarked. 'Look at Tarquin,' she said, pointing to her brother, who was in his own little mad world on the dance floor.

'I agree it does seem against nature's way to see British boys actually moving their feet on a dance floor.'

Then I leaned back in the banquet and inhaled the heady scent of smoke and *la dolce vita* into my lungs. I had been feeling an odd mix of emotions that night; it was wonderful being entertained by so many fit boys. Then again, I felt odd about Malcolm being there and *molto* guilty about Freds being ill. Tarquin assured me as Malcolm had that all Freds had was a nasty chill, but still the guilts are hard to shift once they get a grip.

Then Malcolm came up, and without so much as a by-your-leave, kissed me. Right out of the blue, no warning whatsoever, just like that, he wrapped his lips against mine and got on with it.

Talk about frightening a girl. Admittedly, I rather enjoyed it when he kissed me in Windsor, well up until Freds fell in the Thames, anyway. But that was then, in the context of making Freds jealous. This was now, under the watchful gaze of the British national fencing team, my nuns, Bell End, Biffy and Fizz Whiz – not to mention the Eades Film Society. It was the very apex of mal-ness.

'Hang on a minute,' I told him, disengaging from his clinch. 'What in the name of lip-gloss are you up to?'

'I rather thought I was kissing you.'

'Yes, well, I don't know what the rules are amongst you

Scottish film types, but in the real world you don't just go round kissing girls without a by-your-leave.'

Malcolm didn't look in the least bit chastened. 'What the hell is a by-your-leave, anyway?' he asked.

'Yes, I've always wondered about that,' added Orlando, tapping the ash from his cigarette in the ashtray. 'Is it an old highway code or a Shakespearean whatsit?'

That set the whole table off on an in-depth debate on the linguistic origins of 'by-your-leave.'

'Is that even the point?' I asked the table.

Malcolm, who now had his back to me, turned as if he'd only just noticed I was there. 'What?' he asked.

Well, what's a girl to do? I asked myself. So I stood up to leave. I could see Portia waving at me in the distance. Malcolm had turned back to the debate, which was getting highbrow, with Greek translations flying through the air like croissants at Sunday breakfast. I marched off in a stroppish sort of way to see Portia.

'Seriously, Portia, sometimes I wonder if boys are worth the effort. You won't believe what Malcolm just did.'

'Tell me later. We've got a problem with Jenny. She's totally wasted. Alison is holding her head out of the toilet bowl as we speak. I just walked in and found her there with her head down the loo. I swear I thought she was going to drown. And she's asked specifically for you. Can you take over while I have a quiet word with Bell End. I mean, The Commodore will go spare if he finds out.'

'We can't let Biffy or Bell End know that Jenny's drunk!'

I blurted, and then wondered why. I mean, who was Bell End to judge? I thought as I spotted him at the front of a conga line consisting of a large part of our fencing party, with Biffy taking up the tail end. Talk about letting our side down. Here we were in the capital of style behaving like Basingstoke chavs. It was too *pazzo* for words. 'I don't think he'll be much use,' I added.

'I see what you mean,' Portia agreed, having witnessed what I had. 'Well, come in and help anyway.'

Jenny was, as Portia had warned, head down in the loo, which was not one of those squat jobbies, thank God. She was totally châteaued, mortalled, wasted, bladdered, or to put it more plainly, revoltingly drunk. We may have been sworn enemies, but every girl has a duty to every other girl when it comes to this sort of thing.

'Hi,' I said to Alison. 'I'm Calypso.' They were probably the first words I'd uttered to her, which spoke volumes about my commitment to bonding with my fellow teammates. Still, what better way to bond than sharing the load of sobering up a drunk teammate, I told myself.

'Yeah, I know. You're the girl that's going out with that Prince Freddie. I read about you.'

'Yaah, well, *was* going out with Prince Freddie,' I corrected her, feeling a bit of a lump form in my throat. 'Anyway, let me take over for a bit. We've got to get some water into her.'

'I'll go get that,' Portia said, and left Alison and me to it.

'Good thing tomorrow ain't the tournament. She's going to feel like death.'

I signalled my agreement with a nod as I pulled Jenny's head out of the bowl. Her eyes were closed and her head was lolling. She looked rough. 'Jenny?' I said her name to check if she was conscious. It's a trick I learned from watching old episodes of *Beverly Hills 90210*. Whenever someone was drunk or on drugs, their friends would all repeat their name over and over. Sometimes they even slapped them across the face, an idea I nobly pushed aside.

All Jenny did was moan.

'I don't think she's in a good place,' Alison said as she passed me a wad of wet loo paper.

I wiped Jenny's face and told her, 'You've got to get some water down you, Jenny,' even though she wasn't in any state to understand.

I tried not to show it, but I was actually afraid for her. I mean, people died of alcohol poisoning, didn't they? At least that's what they told us in Special Studies. Jenny looked desperately unwell. The only other people I'd seen drunk were Honey, and Star's dad and his mates, but even they had never been drunk like this. Well, no, that's not true. Tiger was often unconscious.

Portia came in with the water and we managed to get Jenny to drink some. Jenny slurred my name, which I took as a good sign. Italian girls were coming in and out and the word 'mal' was being bandied about with much abandon. I know it sounds shallow, but I was feeling embarrassed about sitting on the floor holding my drunk anti-girlfriend's hair out of her face while her head lolled in the toilet bowl. It didn't paint me in that *la dolce vita* light I was aiming for. Portia had said we were representing our country, and this wasn't how I wanted to represent England or America, or Outer Mongolia for that matter.

'I told Bell End,' Portia said once Jenny had finished drinking the water. 'Well, he's going to find out, isn't he?' she added when she saw the look of horror on my face. 'He's gone off to the pensione. Apparently he's got some sachets of electrolytes there.'

'I don't think we should be giving her *more* drugs,' I whispered sternly.

'They're not drugs,' Alison said helpfully. 'They're sort of like mineral salts. They'll bring her mineral levels back up.'

'We don't want her bringing anything else up, animal, vegetable or mineral,' I said as Jenny put her arms around my neck and told me she loved me. I reluctantly let her nuzzle my face for a bit before allowing her head to droop into my lap. She smelt of toilet water.

Portia and Alison left me alone with her – Alison to tell some Italian boy she'd pulled what was happening, and Portia to get more water. I was left alone with Jenny, who was quite sweet when she was drunk, really. Apart from smelling like toilet water and being cross-eyed. At least she wasn't death staring me.

I stroked her hair and said some nice soothing things,

and then she started to laugh. 'Sucked in!' she cried, sitting up as straight as you like. Then she punched the air triumphantly with her fist.

I stopped my soothing talk and death stared her, but all she did was shrug. 'I just wanted to see how far I could take it. No biggie.'

'Erm, take what, exactly?'

'You and your stuck-up friend. Lady High and Mighty. Think you're all that with your entourage of Eades boys flying out to play with you.'

I was wrong. Jenny was as bad as Honey. Maybe even worse. Not even Honey would stoop to sticking her head in a toilet bowl for attention. Like Delilah cutting off Samson's hair, Honey would get someone else to do it for her.

I stood up as imperiously as I could, walked over to the basin and washed my hands. Then I stepped over Jenny and all her mal-ity and left the loo. Let her deal with Bell End, Portia, Alison and the rest of the team and grown-ups, who were no doubt running themselves into a conga line of feverish madness to save the situation.

I passed Portia as I walked through the club. I took the water from her hands and walked back into the loo and threw it over Jenny. Then I grabbed Portia's hand and led her out, briefly filling her in on our anti-girlfriend's pathetic scheme.

'So what should we do?' Portia asked. 'I mean, Bell End's having kittens. He's charged off back to the pensione for electrolytes and . . .'

'I'll tell you what we'll do. We can leave Jenny to sort out her own drama and enjoy ourselves. I'm going to pull Malcolm and you're going to pull Billy.'

'But we've broken up.'

'Only in England. We're in Italy now, the country of good food, good clothes and good loving.'

Then I walked up to the table where Malcolm et al. were still debating the origins of 'by-your-leave.' And without a by-your-leave or a how's-your-father, I unceremoniously sat on Malcolm's lap and kissed his lips off.

TWENTY-NINE

The City of Amore
and Melodramas!

While kissing Malcolm was pure *la dolce vita* and I should have floated home on a cloud of bliss, I couldn't help taking a wicked pleasure in Jenny's downfall. I still stunk of toilet water. I have no idea what Malcolm must have thought, but either he was too polite to say or couldn't smell me over the fog of his own smoke. I was glad I took Portia's advice on spurning that particular vice.

When the fencing team found out about Jenny's prank, there was an unspoken agreement that she must be sent to Coventry. Dear little Sister Regina couldn't get her lovely nunnish head around Jenny's motivation for pretending to be drunk.

'She's more Honeyesque than any of us realised,' I explained to her as we tottered back to the pensione that evening.

'Oh but Calypso dear, what a nasty, mean trick. I'm sure

I just can't understand such wickedness, child,' Sister Regina murmured while fingering her way through her rosary.

Sister Bethlehem was snoring happily, slung over Bell End's shoulder in her now familiar fireman's lift. She didn't contribute to the discussion per se, but I'm sure she'd have been devastated had she been awake. Nuns aren't built for such worldly wickedness.

Portia and I heard Jenny getting told off in the courtyard as we were preparing for bed, and we stuck our heads out the window so we didn't miss the brouhaha. Biffy warned her that 'another stunt like that, Frogmorten, and you'll be off the team. Quick smart!'

Then Bell End had a go at her. 'Yer bloody idiot, Frogmorten. What did want to pull a stunt like that for? Eh? Eh? You're part of the Great British fencing machine, yer big girl's blouse. We're 'ere, in Italy, playing the game of games! And you're fooling around like a bloody toddler with its nappy over its head!'

And then Biffy started off on a four-year rantarama about how he wouldn't tolerate insubordination in his ranks. Portia and I got bored at that point and fell asleep.

The next morning all the grown-ups had hangovers, which was très, très funny. Oh, how we laughed. Especially at Biffy, who, far from being on patrol at six, didn't surface until ten! He even had the nerve to complain to the Signora that her knife made too much noise scraping the butter onto his toast. She gave him a look that would melt any knife.

The nuns weren't up when we left. Bell End thought it best not to disturb them in case they got upset. I sincerely doubted we'd see Sister Bethlehem's eyes open again for the rest of our stay. But anyway it was not *permisso* to have spectators at the pools.

Even though the salle didn't look far away on the map we studied at breakfast, Bell End had a go at Biffy for being disorganised and not arranging transport. But Portia and I were delighted to be exploring the streets of Florence. Apart from having to lug our fencing kit over three million miles.

Bell End roared when Jenny moaned.

'What's the matter with you, yer big girl's blouse? Yer young, you can take a knock.'

I actually think he had a point. I loved strolling through the streets – kit or no kit. It was like being in a museum of beautiful people and designer shops. As we walked across the Ponte Alle Grazie bridge, Portia and I stopped to lean over the Arno River and scream out mad things. I don't know what it is about bridges and mountains. They just seem to have that effect on young minds, don't they? Perhaps it was brought on by the shop-fest on the Ponte Vecchio bridge opposite, where finest designer delights of the world nestled tightly against the river, awaiting the most awesomely sophisticated shoppers outside of Milano.

While we had our heads down, I asked Portia about Billy, hoping for a straight answer. All she did was smile enigmatically, which set us off chortling like mad things again. Billy and some of the boys caught up with us and asked us what was so funny.

'Just the foolish madness of teenage girls,' I told Billy while Portia composed her blushes.

The boys Billy was hanging out with were quite nice for a bunch of shorties. One was an épéeist and the other two were on the boys' sabre team like him.

'That Jenny's a bit of a lunatic?' one of them remarked conversationally, but no one said anything. I, for one, was over Jenny, although she'd already had a go at me at breakfast about using all the hot water. We mostly talked about Bell End and Biffy and argued the merits of their respective levels of madness, and then we mused about what the Italian team would be like. Probably fearsomely brilliant.

I found our developing camaraderie magical.

As we walked along, Billy and Portia paired off, and as I watched them chatting away together and pointing out buildings and fountains to one another, I couldn't help thinking how sweet they looked. Billy blond and fit as all get-out and Portia with her aristocratic features and rich chocolaty tresses – they were a match made in heaven. Well, made in Windsor at least.

The salle was beside a Medici chapel, and something about the decaying beauty of the building made me walk more reverently. The Italian team was already there doing stretches, but that didn't stop the Italian boys from ooh-la-la-ing the English girls' team as we wandered in.

'*Pappagaillo* alert,' Portia whispered to me. 'Parrots,' she explained.

'But what are they saying?'

'The usual.' She shrugged. 'How beautiful we are, what lovely figures we have, that sort of thing.'

'Oh, aren't they sweet!' I squealed.

Portia shook her long brown tresses. 'No!'

But as a freakishly tall blonde with fluffy little horns of hair that won't stick down however much gel, wax or other fixative I use, I take my compliments where I can.

Then my eyes clapped onto our old fencing master, Professor Sullivan; the most sauvé, debonair gentleman in the fencing world. I nudged Portia, and gave Professor Sullivan a little wave. He smiled and nodded, but that was all. He was always very minimal in his gestures, so I didn't take his lack of hoorahs to heart. Still, I wanted to run up to him and gush about how we'd won our place on the British national team and how Star had chucked fencing for her music, but Professor Sullivan wasn't one for idle gushing. From the looks of things, he was coaching the Italian team now, which meant we were the enemy, so I wandered aloofly alongside Portia and reigned in my gushing side.

I figured Bell End would puff himself up and go *mano a mano* with his predecessor, but I think he was too hung-over, because he just slumped on the first bench he came to. Biffy went over, though, and the two shook hands amiably.

The British team members peeled off into their respective changing rooms to get kitted up.

'Okay, now I am nervous,' Portia told me as we opened our assigned lockers. Then she did the most uncharacteristic jig.

'I know, and can you believe Professor Sullivan is here?'

'I used to have the most enormous crush on him,' she confided. 'I'm worried that my nerves will throw my game.'

'Was I the only girl on the fencing team not to have a crush on Professor Sullivan?' I asked, and then for some unfathomable reason we chortled madly until we both felt sick. You had to be there, really.

We stopped our laughing when Jenny walked in. Not just because she sneered at us. She's one of those girls who has the ability to suck the fun out of a room. I know you're probably asking yourself how much fun can there possibly be in a girls' changing room – even in Florence. But you'd be surprised. Changing rooms are where you say all those confidential girlie things and get to check out one another's knickers and bras – not in a pervy way – just so you can check you're *en trend*. Also, it was our first Italian changing room and we were all talking in Italian accents, which sounded feverishly sophisticated. I would have to remember to ask the 'rents if there was any Italian blood in our Kentucky/English lineage – the Kellyisimos, perhaps?

The trick to speaking Italian – or rather sounding like you speak Italian – is to accentuate or add a vowel on the ends of words, like 'telephona' and 'lippo-glosso.' Within about ten minutes of practice, I swear no one would ever know we weren't born and bred in Florence. Which was a bit worrying actually, because I didn't want anyone mixing our teams up. Luckily we had *GBR* emblazoned on our kit.

It was *molto* exciting changing into our GBR fencing gear for our very first international match. Oh yes, before Jenny walked in, the room was packed to the rafters with *la dolce vita*.

'Oh my God, did you see how fitisimo those boys out there were?' Alison said in her newfound Italian accent.

'Italian boys do seem to have a genetically higher fitisimo level than English boys,' I agreed in my own excellent accent. 'But I don't think it lasts,' I added sagely. 'Did you see those chubby old chappos with their medallions at the discothèque last night?'

'I don't mean the Italian boys. I mean those Eades boys out there filming,' she said – completely out of accent.

Jenny groaned. 'You're all so stupid,' she sneered.

'You mean *stupido*,' I corrected her.

'Idiots,' she sneered lamely.

I decided she wasn't worth wasting our accents on.

We all agreed to walk out into the salle together. Portia had braided my hair like a horse's tail, so I did a bit of a trot. All of us looked sleek and groomed. Even Jenny Frogmorton was looking spiffy.

As I pushed open the door to the salle, I walked straight into Malcolm's camera.

'Ow!' I cried, holding my nose.

'Bugger, sorry, darling, sorry.'

But before I could give him a piece of my passionate Italian mind, the Italians all started applauding us. The girls and boys and even Professor Sullivan were all in an orderly line, clapping for us like we were superstars. I knew it was only the team because they didn't allow any spectators at the pools, but still it was flattering and made us feel welcome and loved.

I forgot about my sore nose and gave our fans a little wave as I walked as elegantly as possible onto the piste.

Biffy blew his whistle, and then for no reason at all, Bell End blew his. Officially, Bell End was only here to chaperone Portia and myself, but unofficially I figured he had scores to settle. He usually did.

'On behalf of the Italian National Under Eighteens team, we'd like to welcome our friends from Great Britain,' Professor Sullivan announced, first in English and then in Italian. Then he bowed ever so slightly. Now there was a man who had élan. Not a single loon-cell in his brain. I hoped Bell End was taking notes.

I set about doing my warm-up stretches and tried to ignore Malcolm's lens, which remained fixed on me the entire time. It was *molto, molto* off-putting, I can tell you.

Eventually Biffy and Professor Sullivan called out the names for the pools and directed players to their respective pistes. It was hard not to be aware of Malcolm's camera, glued as it was to moi. So much for his claim that he wanted footage of Billy.

My first opponent's name was Carlotta. She had a slightly androgynous beauty, as if she'd just walked out of a Caravaggio painting. She had perfect raven curls that hung loose around her shoulders and eyelashes so long they could have been weapons in their own right.

'Ciao,' she said, and I ciaoed her back as we each wired the other up and checked that our electrics were working. 'How you say, good luck?' she asked, batting her lashes for Italy.

'Erm, well, good luck, actually! Or bon chance,' I joked. She looked at me like I was *pazzo*.

I was morbidly conscious that I towered over her like some freakish white bird. She was a good foot and a half shorter than me, and I remembered Bell End's barbed remark about Biffy – the bigger the target, the more there is to hit.

Professor Sullivan was presiding over the bout, and so it was his job to call 'play.' Back when he taught us at Saint Augustine's he always spoke French. But now he called us to the *en guard* lines in his sauvé 1930s English accent. I suspected it was a secret code for, 'Good luck, my country-men and women.'

Carlotta and I saluted. My salute was the usual English casual tipping of my blade, but Carlotta actually kissed her blade and slashed it in a feverishly stylish and slightly terrifying way. The noise cut through my soul like ice as the realization hit me – I was representing Great Britain. I wasn't equipped. I didn't have a fancy salute. I wasn't even British!

We masked up and 'Pretes! Allez! Avanti!' was called.
My Caravaggio opponent advanced down the piste like
a demon. Her footwork was faultless and even before she
lunged I knew I was out of my league. Though I tried to
summon the spirit of Jerzy Pawlowski, the greatest sabreur
who ever lived, all I heard from the president was '*Priorite
a ma droit*,' which means priority to my right. I must 'fess
up and tell you there were ever so few '*Priorite a ma gauche.*'

I was *gauche* . . . in more ways than one.

Actually, I was fencing very well. It was just that
Carlotta was blindingly good. She was in a league of
point and priority grabbing excellence such as I'd never
witnessed. At the end of play when she tore off her mask,
spraying the sweat from her hair everywhere, all I could
do was say, 'Bloody hell, Carlotta, you're good. I mean,
bene.'

She beamed, not smugly, not grandly. She just looked
happy to hear my praise and of course for her win. I
beamed back. Not even sweaty hair could dim her
Renaissance loveliness. I looked over at Malcolm. His
camera was still glued to his face, the lens still fixed on me,
but I wondered, was he comparing Carlotta and me? I
know I was. Freakishly tall, pale blonde girl versus volup-
tuous, stunning, glowing brunette.

And then I wondered something else. Was I jealous?

Over the course of the next two hours, I won a few bouts
and lost a few more. I barely performed well enough to
survive the cull from the pools, but I did survive. That

meant I would get to play in the tournament tomorrow. Unlike Jenny, who had been culled.

I know it was shallow of me, but it made me feel that justice existed after all. Sometimes, bad things do happen to mean girls.

Professor Sullivan came over afterwards and asked, 'So how does it feel to be on the national team, Miss Kelly?' – only he asked in French of course.

'Yaah, it's really cool, basically, but these girls are, like . . . Well they're really, really good, aren't they? Do you think I can ever be that good?' I asked in my best approximation of a French accent.

And then he smiled. It was a smile that lit up the entire salle, and then something miraculous happened. He spoke to me in English for the first time ever. 'Most definitely, Calypso. Without a shadow of a doubt, in fact. There is one thing I have always had infinite faith in, and that is your ability to be as good as you want to be.'

THIRTY

He Made It Seem Like the Most Sensible Thing in the World . . .

As we came out of the salle, Malcolm grabbed my hand and pulled me aside.

'Can we talk?'

I looked down at his hand holding mine, but I didn't pull it away. I was feeling high and positive, and actually it felt rather nice, especially when he took my shoulder-biting fencing kit from me and put it on his own shoulder.

'What's up?' I asked, but all he did was pull me behind the old Medici church and kiss me long and hard. I know when boys kiss you you're meant to go off to a dreamy cloudland of magical warmth and loveliness, but I have that sort brain that never switches off. I couldn't help comparing Malcolm's kissing to Freds'. Which was totally wrong and shallow, I know. But Malcolm's pulling style was *molto* passionate.

Kissing Freds was cloudlandy. At the time, I always thought it the apex of loveliness, but it was different to kissing Malcolm. Malcolm took a strand of my wet hair and placed it behind my ear and smiled. I ruffled his red hair and looked into his luminous green eyes and studied his face. Just as I was memorising it, he locked his lips on mine and did that dip thing again.

Suddenly he pulled me up as a priest was walking past. He said hello to the young priest in Italian and they had a short chat. I nodded and smiled and laughed when they laughed, but they may well have been discussing trigonometry.

Eventually Father went off to do a spot of shopping – well, that was my assessment – and Malcolm turned his mega-watt personality back onto me. 'I need your help,' he told me seriously.

I thought he wanted to kiss me again and puckered up.

'No, seriously. I think I've found the perfect subject for the film I came here to make.'

'I thought you came here to film Billy.'

'Did I tell you that?'

'Yes.'

He ran his hands through his hair, and for a moment he reminded me of Freds – an older, strawberry-blond, more eccentric Freds. 'I wonder if that's what I meant to do. Anyway, something happened this morning. I have to show it to you; I want your opinion. It was the maddest thing, really – the way it all came about. I went off this morning to get my nipple pierced and –'

'Wait, why did you get your nipple pierced?' I asked, trying to keep all judgment from my mind as I remembered my own navel-piercing fiasco in Los Angeles last summer.

'Eyebrow piercing is so passé,' he said, as if this should be all the explanation I deserved. Boys! 'And well, only hippies and bikers do their ears or lips, don't they?'

'I suppose,' I replied, quite glad he hadn't said anything about navel piercing being passé.

'And on consideration I'm pretty certain the madre would have an embolism if I pierced my face. I did consider a wrist piercing, but only briefly. The chap who did the deed, nice guy, bit of a freak, but anyway point is, he had his wrist pierced. It was the darndest of darn things. I've never considered piercing my wrist before. But I'm not sure it wouldn't become a bit of a nuisance, you know with cuffs and all that.' Then he started looking at old footage in his video camera.

'But I don't understand why you had to get anything pierced?' I told him.

'What?' he looked up. Clearly he'd completely lost the thread of the conversation.

'Why get anything pierced?'

He appeared to consider this for a while. 'I see what you're saying. I hadn't thought of it that way, but anyway, the point is, look, let me show you –'

I took a step back. 'Take it away. I don't want to see your nipple!' I squealed. I like to think I'm a girl made of strong American fibre, but I was not a studier of fresh nipple piercings – or old ones for that matter. Star, Georgina and I had had our navels pierced last summer. It was a bonding sort of thing. But mine had gone septic, and Sarah had made me take it out after a showdown with the poor guy who'd performed the deed. No, I was off body piercing for life.

Malcolm ruffled my hair and laughed. 'I wasn't going to show you my nipple,' he assured me. 'Besides, I bottled out at the last minute.' Then he grabbed my hand and insisted I come with him to see something 'incredibly cool.'

Incredibly cool, incredibly cool. I kept repeating the phrase to myself as he dragged me through the bright winter streets of Florence. I couldn't stop wondering, what in algebra's name would a boy like Malcolm consider 'incredibly cool'? Not cool, mind you, but *incredibly* cool.

'Is it a really amazing Renaissance painting? I know, we're going to the Uffizi to see the Botticelli room?'

He laughed. 'That's in the other direction. Just wait and see.'

'I know, a vinyl shop? We're going to a vinyl shop so you can buy old eighties recordings of tragic, I mean cool, Italian bands no one else has heard of.' Star told me that boys love obscure indie bands they imagine no one else has heard of. But then Malcolm wasn't most boys.

'No,' he told me firmly. 'Just wait and see.'

And then I saw a cinema in the distance. 'I know, I know. It's an arty Italian movie?' Oh yes, that seemed likely.

'No.' He pulled me along faster. 'Just wait, we're almost there.' We turned down a dark, narrow lane where we passed a shop that sold motor scooter parts and then a shop that did tattoos and body piercing. Malcolm waved to the guy inside, whose entire body was glinting with piercings. I began to hyperventilate, but we didn't stop there, thank goodness.

'I know, you've discovered an amazing crumbling-down old building that a mad dead Medici lived in. Everyone's forgotten about it and stopped searching. But you've found it, all vine-covered, and you alone have realised what it really is, and you've started–'

'You really should become an author, Calypso. Your imagination needs a larger canvas.'

Of course I was madly flattered and started walking on air. Freds had never even noticed my creative spirit. He just thought I was mad. I made a mental note to tell Miss Topler that my mind needs a larger canvas than her class.

'We're here,' Malcolm said, gesturing to a shop front. 'Now you can satisfy your curiosity to your heart's delight.'

We were standing outside a pet shop. I looked at Malcolm's face, but his eyes were fixed on something inside. I mean, I'm as keen on pets as the next girl, but as you can't bring animals into the UK without inserting microchips into their ears and getting them special pet passports. It's not really the sort of shop you'd look out for a souvenir. Well, I don't. I worry I'd fall in love with a kitten or puppy or a hamster, and then it would be an awful wrench, knowing I couldn't take it home with me.

I wasn't wildly keen on going inside and finding something too cute to leave behind, so I said, 'So what, it's just a pet shop. That's hardly incredibly cool. They're everywhere.'

Malcolm jerked me inside. 'Look,' he said, pointing to a large wooden crate that was full of tiny paper boxes that looked a bit like Chinese takeaway boxes. They were all open and empty apart from one box where a tiny little black-speckled duckling was franticly flapping and peeping.

'Oh bless!' I exclaimed.

'When I came in here this morning to contemplate the piercing, every one of these cartons here was full of ducklings. I stood here and filmed as customer after customer came into the shop and bought a duckling. I was here for, oh, I don't know, about an hour.' He then spoke to the pet shop owner in Italian.

The guy replied without looking up from his newspaper.

'Yes, Giuseppe thinks it was a bit over an hour. And in that time, every other duckling was sold. Except for this little chap.'

The tiny duckling had his miniature bill in the air. He appeared to be looking and talking directly at us. '*Peep,*

peep, peep, peep!' Honestly, it was the most adorable sight I had ever seen. Even Dorothy wasn't as cute as the duckling, which made me feel disloyal just to think such a thought.

'Can we hold him?' I asked Giuseppe in my best Italian accent. But Giuseppe didn't seem to understand my wonderful Italianised English.

Malcolm asked the owner in Italian for me, but I could tell the answer was no because of all the head shaking and arm waving that went on.

'Apparently he won't let us because last month someone picked up one of his ducklings and dropped it on the floor and broke its wing,' Malcolm translated.

All the while the little duckling was going *'peep, peep, peep.'*

'But I don't understand. Why didn't anyone buy him? He's adorable.'

'Yaah, I agree,' Malcolm said as he filmed the duckling peeping piteously. 'They don't like his mottled colours, apparently.'

'Oh, that's soooo mean. That's what gives him his character.'

Malcolm was taking some close-up footage as he replied. 'I agree.'

I couldn't bear it. I really couldn't bear it. The duckling wouldn't stop peeping and flapping its stunted little wings. Where was its mother? Where were its friends? Where was its pond to play in? It was horrible and I was powerless to help, so I ran out of the shop and down the lane.

Malcolm caught up with me and hugged me tightly into his chest. 'Sorry, I didn't mean to upset you. See, I'm stuck and need your help. I wanted to do a short of all the customers frantically scooping up their ducks and buying them, but then when no one scooped up Rex – that's what I've named him, by the way – it went from being an art-house documentary to a tragedy.'

'What do you mean?'

I can't show this on Film Night at Eades. Everyone would walk out in despair. No, I need to find a happy ending. Someone has to buy that duckling. I've paid the guy for Rex already and said he can offer him for free. So, hopefully when we come back tomorrow he'll be sold.'

I clung to Malcolm like I clung to the hope that Rex would find his home. I felt so emotional. Not just because I was touched by the plight of Rex, but because I was touched that Malcolm had taken me to the pet shop. I was touched that he wanted to share the whole thing with me. He was not your ordinary boy. I mean, of course I already knew that, but now I could hear Star egging me on. Saying, 'Go for it, Calypso, he's so the one.'

Maybe she was right. Unlike Freds, Malcolm was anything but ordinary.

THIRTY-ONE

The End of the Beginning and the Beginning of the End

That evening was a quiet one. Jenny went to bed in a strop. 'That bloody Italian cheated, and that wanker of a president saw it,' she railed.

'Professor Sullivan sees everything,' Portia told her, her black eyes flashing. 'He's the most upright man you're ever likely to meet.'

Jenny flounced out of the room muttering obscenities. 'I think I almost prefer Honey,' I told Portia later. 'At least she's a worthy combatant.'

'You just think that because Honey's hundreds of miles away, Calypso. It's like in that song, "If you can't be with the one you hate, hate the one you're with."'

Portia can be *molto* wise. Probably all those generations of inbreeding.

We went to bed early, leaving the nuns to play cards

with Bell End and Signora. In the morning we showered and bathed and made ourselves look *molto* gorgeous for the tournament. Except for Jenny, who exuded horribleness. Even though she'd been culled, Biffy was making her attend the tournament to boost team spirit. Spectators were allowed today, so the nuns were up at breakfast, bright-eyed with excitement.

'Signora helped make a banner,' Sister Regina announced proudly as she and Sister Bethlehem held up a white tablecloth.

'But Sisters, there's nothing written on it,' I said, hating to be the one to burst their bubble. Poor mad little things.

The Sisters exchanged a knowing look, at least I think that's what it was. It's hard to tell with those big thick spectacles. Then they turned their cloth around, which took a while because they kept getting twisted up in it. But eventually the reverse side was displayed.

The words GREAT BRITAIN RULES THE PISTE were painted professionally in red and blue paint.

Portia and I gave them a cuddle.

Bell End said, 'That's the spirit, Sisters, we'll show them.' Then he turned to us. 'Right, girlies, today's the day you rend the flesh from the bones of the fascist Italian witches. No backbone, these Italians, see, no front bone for that matter. A bunch of big girls' floral blouses with bows on them. No, Great Britain will wipe the salle with their Italian blood. They can bloody well go home and cry in the bosoms of their mothers.'

'Mr Wellend, I think you'll find this is *their* home. We're what's known as the visiting team,' The Commodore explained, laughing into his walrus moustache.

'Not for long, Biff, not for long. Fencing's not a game, as well you know, my old comrade. It's war! Yesterday we let them think we were a bunch of wets. Well, not today! Not today. If blood must be spilled, better theirs than ours is what I say. To your arms, girls, to your arms!' he yelled – and then he blew his whistle.

'Okay, thank you, Mr Wellend, most colourful,' Biffy responded patronisingly. 'But I think you'll find I'm the manager here, and well, to strike a more instructive note, let's just say, may the best team win.'

God I hated him.

Bell End wasn't going to have Biffy pop his mad balloon, though. 'Have their guts for garters!' he cried, and we all punched the air with our fists and cheered.

Jenny said, 'God, you are soooo stupid.'

'You're the bloody idiot that got knocked out in the pools, yer big girl's blouse,' Bell End reminded her.

The boys from the Eades Film Society were waiting for us at the salle where the beautiful Carlotta and her teammates were ready to rinse us. Malcolm was there filming away, and I gave him a little wave. I put on a brave face, which fortified me a bit, but the calibre of these girls was the alpha and omega of perfection – and I don't just mean their looks.

As we started our stretches, a mighty roar erupted from

the Eades boys, which made me blush. Then they started on a series of chavie football chants.

'Eng-ga-land! Eng-ga-land!'

As play was called for the first match, their cries intensified to include classic hits of the football stadiums.

It was soooo embarrassing. Especially when I lost my bout.

As I saluted my opponent in the next bout, I went into a zanshin – a samurai swordsman state of being. Zanshin is a state of mind of complete action when there is no time to take back or fix a stroke or a stride. Zanshin means going beyond technique, because you can't force your opponent to conform to your moves in the way you want. The angle and force of a strike must be adjusted immediately to the energy of your opponent.

I emptied my mind of the English cheer squad. I emptied my mind of Freds and Malcolm and the duckling and asked for divine guidance.

Professor Sullivan and Bell End had two very different styles. Professor Sullivan was all about speed and efficiency and the physical game of chess. Bell End was more a slam 'em with your blade and rain on their parade sort of guy. I wondered what would happen if I drew on both styles for inspiration. As 'play' was called, I was psyched for an aggressive game of chess.

I scored my first hit with a classic Professor Sullivan manoeuvre: advancing down the piste in a seemingly obvious attack by threatening my opponent with a cut to the head. This provoked her into a parry of quinte. I rotated my blade to score an effortless cut to her flank. The point was mine, and we returned to the *en guard* line. As I'd hoped, my opponent's mind ran along predictable lines, which I used to my advantage throughout the game.

The bout was mine. As I was being wired up for my next bout, I ignored my aching muscles and throbbing bruises and remained totally zanshin. I kept up the game of bluff and double bluff, going in for the aggressive attack only to slay her with an unexpected manoeuvre. Professor Sullivan had always been big on wrist action, and I used the adroit strength of my wrists to full advantage that day.

As I made my way back to the *en guard* line between each point, I was vaguely aware of Bell End blowing his whistle while running up and down the various pistes like a madman. I closed my mind and went back to my zanshin state so that his violent instructions to 'slay the filthy witches' would fall on deaf ears.

I won each bout using the same Professor Sullivan/Bell End combination of tactics. Yet despite my own personal victories, ultimately the Great British team was proclaimed the loser.

I know this probably sounds like I'm not a team player, but actually I didn't feel that bad about losing our first international match, because something extraordinary had happened to me on the Italian piste that day. I had metamorphosed into a totally different sabreur than the one who had left England just two days before. By fusing the finesse of Professor Sullivan with the brutality of Bell End I had developed the ability to deliver a ferocious onslaught on the head of a pin. The speed and ferocity of the Italians had taught me that Bell End was right; you needed a lot of aggression to be a sabreur. But Professor Sullivan was right as well; your aggression had to be tempered with precise manoeuvres and intellectual finesse. The British team had lost this time, but I'd played well. Next time we'd wipe the floor with our opponents.

The Italians shook hands graciously and insisted on taking us out to dinner that night. In the changing rooms afterwards, the girls were *molto* charming and gave us a great deal of help with our Italian accents. Even sentences like 'my hair is soooo sweaty' sounded sexy with an Italian accent. When we returned to Saint Augustine's, everyone would think we were Italian goddesses.

After changing, we all went our separate ways. Billy and Portia were off to the Duomo and to do some shopping on the Vecchio. Malcolm took me behind the Medici chapel for another snog-age.

'You were amazing,' he told me, and then he gave me another soulful kiss. 'What on earth happened to you on the piste today? You were like a storm of avenging angels, darling. You really are unpredictable and full of surprises, Calypso Kelly.'

Freds was always telling me that I was full of surprises too. But when he said it, he made it sound like a bad thing. The way Malcolm said it made me feel interesting, mysterious and jam-packed with undiscovered possibilities.

So I kissed him in a very unpredictable way.

THIRTY-TWO

The Italian Duckling Job

As we burst into the pet shop, Giuseppe put down the paper he'd been reading and shook his head. My prayers to Mary, Saint Francis of Assisi (the patron saint of animals) and every other saint I knew the name of had gone unanswered. Which is challenging to a young girl's faith, I can tell you that now.

We could hear Rex peeping before we even looked in his carton. He was flapping his little useless wings, and I was almost certain I saw tears in his eyes. 'How can Italians, the great people who have given us philosophers and theologians by the lorry load, be so horrible to a helpless duckling?' I asked Malcolm.

'Jerkism is an international affliction,' he said as he commenced filming.

'Well, I don't think the pope will be too pleased when he hears about this,' I muttered, only very, very softly, because

Malcolm might have been an atheist or an agnostic or even a communist for all I knew.

'Oh, Rex,' I sobbed. 'There you are, pathetically flapping away in your pathetic paper carton, and us helpless to help.' I wanted him to know I felt his pain.

Rex was peeping himself sick while Malcolm filmed him. Giuseppe put down his paper and came over. I could tell that underneath his mustachioed bravado beat the heart of a duckling lover, because he indicated with a flick of his hand that I could cuddle Rex after all.

I was very tentative at first, but Rex practically dived out of my cupped hands, so I clutched him more firmly as I brought him up to my face for a kiss. I swear he was the most adorable duckling in the entire world. I'd seen his lucky evenly coloured peers on Malcolm's video, and none of them, not a one, had his pluck and character. Rex, for all his speckled blotchiness, was a king among ducklings.

His frantic peeping didn't let up. If I could have translated Italian duckling speak, I'd swear he was begging me to take him home. His little beak felt like batting eyelids on my neck and cheeks. It was very tickly, actually, and I started to giggle. Not that I wasn't *molto* moved and despairing. I held him away from my face a bit and looked at him, girl to duck. His little eyes were all wet and pleading.

I turned to Malcolm – well, Malcolm's camera lens – and wondered if he was thinking the same thing: This whole situation was rum.

'This is too awful, Malcolm,' I said.

Malcolm looked at me for a moment. Really looked, but instead of agreeing with me, he had another conversation, in real Italian, with Giuseppe. Next minute we were leaving the shop with our new duckling.

As we strode onto the street, Rex peeping excitedly, I was thinking about what an un-Freddie thing to do. A nasty part of me even thought Freds would be more likely to shoot little Rex than rescue him. But I knew that wasn't true. Still, I wondered, would Freds ever do anything as random as stroll out of a Florence pet shop with a duckling, sans valid duck passport and microchip?

'What will we do?' I asked Malcolm as we headed back up the lane. 'I mean, we can't take Rex back to England. That was the maddest decision we could have made.'

'I know, but aren't those the best decisions to make?' he replied. As we dashed up the lane, it occurred to me that following his flights of fancy was probably something Malcolm did every day. Turning up in Florence like that was a prime example of his eccentric persona. And actually, I liked that about him. As a filmmaker he was bound to be slightly unrealistic, a mad dreamer.

Which was fine for *him*.

In his eccentric Scottish world of endless trust funds, champagne and independence, I guess he could afford to be a dreamer with no grip on reality. But I couldn't. I wasn't Scottish or minted, and I hated champagne. Plus I could hear Bob's voice in my ears – saying in his sternest *pazzo* voice, "Sometimes, Calypso, you go *too* far."

What if my mad padre was right, though? I mean, even a broken clock is right twice a day.

As we wove our way through the streets of Florence, vespas honking at us furiously as we dashed in their path, tourists gawping, café sophisticates smoking and chatting, Rex kept up his chorus of peeps. There would be no way to hide him once we returned to the pensione, and we were flying out tomorrow, anyway. What was Malcolm thinking? I hope he wasn't planning on plopping our little orphan in the Arno to fend for himself.

Maybe this whole duckling rescue was just a plot device for Malcolm's film?

Maybe all he really cared about was a happy ending for *The Last Duckling*?

Maybe I was just incidental. A pleasant distraction in his creative world of plot device and flights of fancy.

Maybe I'd be better off with a nice sensible boy like Freds after all.

These were the questions going through my mind as I scampered through the streets of Florence with a duckling when really I should have been visiting the Uffizi or shopping on the Ponte Vecchio or something sensible like that. I should be writing witty postcards to the 'rentals about my tournament. As it was I visualised a postcard flopping on the mat of chez Clapham as I ran.

Dear Sarah and Bob,
Florence is bellisimo! My fencing has taken on a spiritual
quality – even though we did lose the tournament. Oh, by
the way I've acquired a duckling since I left England and
shall quite possibly be arrested on my attempt to re-enter
England. His name is Rex.
Love, Calypso xxxxxxxxxxxxxxxxxxxxxxxxxxxxxxxxxxxxxxx
    (I went mental with the x's to remind them that I was
their loving daughter, so they wouldn't get cross.)
PS: What do ducklings eat?
PPS: What do ducklings drink?

I was really starting to panic about Malcolm's motiva-
tions now. Why had Freds dumped me? He was nice and
ordinary and at this particular point I was thinking
ordinary is good. I would never have been imprisoned
for duck smuggling if I'd been with Freds. The cobbled
lane was too hard to faint on but lordy, lordy, as my gran
would say, I've never needed a good old faint more than I
needed one that afternoon.

THIRTY-THREE

Aren't the Maddest Ideas Always the Best?

Malcolm and I had our first row a short time later. I shall treasure the memory forever. It took place in a café on the Piazza Santissima Annunziata over double espressos. As settings for arguments go, I can highly recommend this picturesque and noble square on account of its *molto bellisimo* porticoes and church. Also, there is a rather magnifique statue of some bloke on a horse and two fountains on which monkeys dribble water on a couple of sea slugs. Mad.

In addition to being my first argument with Malcolm, it was also my first real row with a boy. Arguing with Freds had always consisted of long periods of him not taking or responding to my numerous calls, txts and e-mails. Fighting with Malcolm involved proper raised voices and the heated exchange of viewpoints.

The fight was over Rex, poor love. First he was stuck in

a Chinese takeaway carton while his peers were snapped up like this season's latest accessory. Then finally, just when he thought he'd found two people to love and care for him, they start brawling about his future smuggling arrangements. And then there was the issue of where he'd live because the thing was, as sophisticated and worldly as this trip had made me, we were still both schoolkids ill-equipped for duckling management.

'Can't he live with you?' Malcolm asked as he lit his fag.

'Are you *mad*?' I shrieked. 'No, don't answer that, because you clearly are quite the nutty one charging off with ducklings like that.'

'It's only the one duckling, Calypso. I don't exactly make a habit of duckling rescue,' he replied. His tone was poisonous with sarcasm, and I felt a bit upset that he managed to look even fitter and more mature as he made his sarcastic remark.

'No, well, I should think not. It's still very irresponsible,' I told him, realising I was sounding like Bob.

'You were the one throwing the Ophelia in the pet shop, darling,' he added. Only he made the word *darling* sound like a nasty insult.

'Well,' I sulked. 'I can't help being a sensitive, feeling person can I?'

'Rex, you are a tug-of-love duckling,' Malcolm told him as he peeped himself stupid in his swaddling napkin.

Ironically we were facing the Spedale degli Innocenti, which was the first-ever orphanage in Europe. Malcolm tried to feed Rex a few crumbs of his biscotti, which I thought proved how ill-equipped he was for parenthood.

'I don't think you should be feeding him biscuits,' I told him, even though Rex seemed delighted. 'They'll rot his teeth.'

'Fine,' Malcolm replied, chucking the biscotti onto the table. Rex looked at me in a pissed-off sort of way.

'Fine,' I replied back, folding my arms and glaring.

So we sat in silence, sipping our espressos, as the sun went down, other couples canoodled and vespas sped past.

Malcolm frowned but he didn't say anything. Then he took back the biscotti and started dropping little crumbs in Rex's beak. It was actually sweet watching Rex eat. His little beak went berserk.

I watched Malcolm holding our little orphan and feeding him crumbs. I already knew he was eccentric, unpredictable and lacking in judgment. So maybe it was a bit unreasonable of me to expect reason, judgment and sanity from Malcolm? Now if Freds were here, he'd know exactly what to do. Then again if Freds were here I wouldn't be sitting here with an orphaned duckling.

Still, Malcolm was being very sweet to Rex, and looking at him I suddenly wanted to pull him. 'I don't want to argue. I'm just worried about how we'll get him through customs,' I explained more gently.

Malcolm looked up at me and smiled. 'Oh, I quite enjoyed our little *contretemps*. Your lips are quite kissable when you're pouting,' he teased, offering me a piece of biscotti to feed Rex. 'Listen, don't be worried. I'm leaving tonight. It's far better that I take him back to England in my hand luggage,' he insisted as he waved to the waiter for another espresso.

'But you can't. The authorities will spot Rex in their X-ray machine thingamees and the poor thing will end up at the mercy of Italian customs officials! I shall do it.'

'Fair enough,' he agreed without a fight. 'You do it.' Then before I could faint with the horror of what I'd just volunteered to do, he kissed me, and people at surrounding tables clapped.

'See, my lovely sabre-wielding wild child, you have me eating out of the palm of your hand.'

On the way back, I decided that Malcolm was not the boy for me even if he did think I was a wild child. He was far too eccentric, even if it was in a creative way. As amusing as he was to be with, life was not a movie set. I needed a nice, normal boyfriend who didn't complicate my life with ducklings and other imponderables. Because now that I'd won the argument over who was taking Rex back, it began to dawn on me what a pyrrhic victory it actually was. I mean, how was I going to smuggle Rex through customs? What if they discovered me and chucked me in Old Chokey and I had to live on gruel and wander an exercise yard with girls who were wise to the ways of crime and flick knives?

I suppose I'd be used to the food at least.

My soul was heavy with all this pondering when

Malcolm eventually said, 'Shall we see if Rex can swim?' And before I could say something cautionary and sensible, he'd dropped him in the fountain.

Rex took to the fountain like a duck to water, but still. 'How could you be so irresponsible!' I screamed. 'What if he'd drowned?'

Malcolm laughed as he picked me up and chucked me in after Rex.

If I had any doubts about whether Malcolm was actually the boy for me, they were drowned in that pool of deadly bacteria.

'Rex,' I told him later after we had gone to Malcolm's grand palazzo to dry off. 'I'm sorry to have to break it to you, but your parents are splitting up.'

Malcolm was drying my hair with one of the big white towels as I broke this shocking news to our duckling child. Rex seemed to take it well. So did Malcolm, which was probably the most *molto* annoying thing about the whole breakup. I know we hadn't officially been going out, but we had adopted a duckling together, and so technically that made him the first boy I'd officially dumped. Only I don't think Malcolm realised this technicality, which was *molto* annoying. When you dump someone, you want to see a certain amount of disappointment.

'I hope you realise that I meant that,' I told him. 'About the being dumped thing.'

'Really?' he asked as he finished drying my hair off. 'Perhaps you should do it by txt? That will show me.'

'Hah!' I said, grabbing the towel and flicking him with it. 'How dare you mock my tragedy!'

And I chased him round the palazzo until we reached the kitchen, where he grabbed me in a manly hug. 'Fancy something to eat, my gorgeous Botticelli angel?' he asked, trying to kiss me.

'Fine!' I replied, pulling away.

So he set to work and whipped up some eggs Fiorentina, which I hate to admit were divinely delicious. I had two servings and then despite myself I had several more servings of Malcolm's delicious lips. 'Don't think that just because I like kissing you we're un-dumped or anything,' I told him sternly.

'Whatever you say, my cherub,' he teased.

It was after eleven when he finally walked me back to the pensione. I let him put his arm around me, but that was only because I was freezing cold. When he tried to kiss me at the door, I pushed him away and delivered my pre-prepared speech. 'I do like you, Malcolm, but we're not suited. I need a nice, normal boy, not a Scottish nipple-piercing filmmaker. This madness is too much for me. It's been a lovely holiday romance, but the time has come to face –'

'Calypso,' he interrupted.

'What?'

Then he pulled me into his chest and gave me the best snog-age I've ever had.

'You do say the most idiotic things. See you in Windsor

on Saturday,' he told me, dashing off into the night. I was still swooning with the dreamy madness of it all as a vespa sped past and almost knocked me off my feet.

I rang the bell of the pensione and waited in the chill night with my swaddled duckling contemplating the Malcolm-versus-Freddie issue. Eventually I was admitted by the night-watch chap.

In the courtyard, Sister Regina and Sister Bethlehem were sipping some petrol – I think the Italians like to call it grappa – with the Signora.

'I'm disappointed in you, Calypso,' Sister Regina said as I entered the courtyard.

I thought she must be referring to Rex, who was peeping away frantically. The idea that tomorrow I was going to successfully smuggle him into Great Britain was madness of the first order. What on earth had possessed me to insist on sole custody of Rex? As a tall, fit boy, surely Malcolm was much better suited to the rigours of Old Chokey than me?

I placed Rex on the table and fell into Sister's arms and sobbed. 'Oh Sister, I didn't know what to do. No one would buy him and Malcolm was filming him and, well, we bought him, and now I don't know how I'm going to smuggle him through customs, and he won't stop peeping, and I'll end up in Old Chokey, and Bob and Sarah will be –'

'Shush, child,' Sister soothed, stroking my hair while Signora Santospirito and Sister Bethlehem clucked away over Rex. 'What's all this? I was talking about you missing the team dinner.'

'Oh no. I can't believe I missed my first post-international tournament team dinner. Will they throw me off the team, Sister?'

'No one's throwing anyone off anything. Though I daresay Mr Wellend and Mr Biffy will give you a steely look or two, but the main worry is drying up these silly tears.'

She dabbed my face with one of her long sleeves. 'Now what's all this about Old Chokey?' she asked.

'Rex.' I pointed. 'I can't leave him here and I can't take him home.'

'I could take him in my sleeve,' Sister Bethlehem suggested.

I looked at her and smiled. Bless. She was so sweet. Daft as socks, but ever so sweet.

'No one would dare look in a nun's sleeve,' Sister Bethlehem assured me.

'That's right,' Sister Regina agreed. 'Not the lowest swine would dare trespass on a nun's sleeve.'

'But someone will hear him,' I reasoned.

'I'll say it's my joints,' Sister Bethlehem told me, and so it was settled.

THIRTY-FOUR

You're No One Until Someone Wants to Sell Stories about You to the Press

I was a bundle of nerves on the flight home, not just because of our smuggling but because each mile was bringing me closer to Freds, and my feelings about him were more jumbled than ever. Sister Regina forced me to drink some brandy to calm myself, but all it did was make me feel sick. Sister Bethlehem slept the whole way, and I had to keep checking on Rex to make sure she didn't crush him. Fortunately the noise of the flight drowned out his incessant peepings, but I was not full of *joie de vivre* as we touched down at Gatwick.

Customs was not at all what I expected. I don't mean the whole smuggling livestock palaver, because that went off without a hitch – walking through the Nothing to

Declare aisle with two nuns was a breeze. Thank you, Saint Jude – patron saint of lost causes – once more, you've come through.

No, the first voice I heard at the other end of the barrier was Honey screaming, 'That's her! That's her! The tall one with fluffy bits sticking out the top of her head. The one in the chav top.'

And then a blaze of flashlights went off in my face.

Blinded, I groped through the noise of a thousand paps clicking their cameras and drowning all thoughts in my mind. You've heard that saying like a deer caught in headlights? Well, that was me. Scared out of my wits. Bell End was right, I was a big girl's blouse.

People were calling out my name and asking me questions. 'So how's it feel to be called the prince's slapper, luv?'

'Is it true you pushed him in the Thames because he dumped you, Calypso?'

'Bitter was you?'

'Were all those things you said true? Did your parents really torture you as a child?'

'Is it true you pulled his best mate, the Laird of Killmarn?'

'What was your Florence love-nest like? Raunchy was it?'

I felt myself being grabbed and groped and began to lash out. Then I made out the shadowy figures of my parents, Sarah and Bob, as I heard them call out to me above the hubbub. My lovely wonderful, protective, much-maligned parents, Sarah and Bob. They grabbed me and I grabbed them like a drowning girl grabbing two life jackets. Suddenly we were surrounded by four blokes in buzz cuts and sharp suits.

'Right, guys, get us out of here,' Bob said with an authority that shocked me to the core.

'But my fencing gear?' I cried – I know, how materialistic. But seriously, you knock yourself out trying to make the national team of your country. You wouldn't let go of the kit either.

'It's all taken care of, darling,' the madre assured me in the tone she used to use when I was ill and allowed to eat egg and soldiers in bed – we're talking four years old here.

The suits led us to the waiting limo as the paps kept up their relentless barrage of questions and flashes.

It was très, très merde with double algebra bells on.

Finally the door of the stretch was slammed shut and the stadium-strength flashlights of the pap's cameras stopped. I could see again. 'What, in the name of old ladies' knickers, is going on?' I asked.

A few indefatigable paparazzi banged on the roof and windows of the limo as we drove away from the curb. Why do they do that? I mean, did they honestly think that I was going to come out and face their prying lenses and obscene questioning?

I guess they did. Hope is a powerful form of delusion. Believe me, I speak from personal experience.

'We thought it best to keep it all from you while you were in Florence,' Bob explained. 'We wanted you to concentrate on your fencing.'

My eyes were still blurry from the flashes that had been blasting my retinas for the last ten minutes, so I was struggling to focus on the buzz cuts sitting opposite us.

'Oh, and who are these guys?' I asked, pointing to the grumpy suits who were eyeing me up like I was a prime suspect.

'We thought you might need some security for a bit,' Bob explained.

'Just until it all blows over,' Sarah added hastily, giving my knee a comforting squeeze.

'Security from what?' I asked. I couldn't help feeling like this was all a practical joke or maybe payback for The Incident when I was three. I swear, I would not put it past my 'rentals to pull a stunt like that to prove a point. They are from Hollywood after all.

'Erm . . . perhaps you'd better read these, Calypso,' Bob suggested as he placed a pile of newspapers on my lap. 'There's a lot more, but that should give you the gist of the situation.'

'Oh,' I replied as the first headline hit me like a lacrosse ball between the eyes. 'Prince's Slapper Claims Parental Abuse!'

This was going to be worse than The Incident – I just knew it. I flicked through the first dozen or so headlines. I'd been accused of purposefully pushing Freds into the

Thames, pulling his 'best mate, the Laird of Killmarn.' Malcolm hadn't said anything about being a laird – whatever a laird was. Oh, and apparently I was a lush to rival all lushes. There was even a snap of me knocking back a cocktail in a nightclub with Honey, presumably taken last term on the weekend she'd famously vomited in my handbag.

Naturally there were loads of quotes from Honey. She'd given a personal account of how she'd desperately tried to prevent my spiralling downfall. Her piece was titled: 'My Friend The Slut!' – the sub read, '*The Honourable Honey O'Hare, It Girl, Socialite and muse to the stars, has kindly donated her fee for this article to the charity ADIG (Alms for Dilapidated It Girls.)*'

Of course she had, darling!

God, I wished Star was here.

But I couldn't blame Honey. The worst of it was that each piece was littered with quotes from my stupid short-listed essay about my mad 'rentals. Had I really written such vitriolic rubbish? It put Nancy Mitford's thinly disguised book about her own family into perspective. I thought it amusing, but most of her family never spoke to her again. One of her other books, *A Talent to Annoy*, came to mind. Perhaps in years to come I would write a book, *A Talent for Dramarama*.

How was I meant to imagine that an essay on my pathetic personal tragedies could make the short list above essays from orphans and refugees and kids with terminal diseases? There were teens out there who had experienced real tragedy.

Over the past week I'd been so preoccupied with Freds dumping me, The Counter Dump, the fall-out of The Counter Dump, the tournament in Florence, Malcolm, and smuggling ducklings that I had totally forgotten about the essay.

Now I was in the merde. I looked at Sarah and Bob as tears of love, compassion, remorse and fear mingled and ran down my face in a river of shame. 'I didn't mean all those things,' I told them. 'Honestly, I did write lots of lovely things about you too. I promise I did,' I ranted. 'But the entry rules limited me to three thousand words, and it had to be about great traumas. I wish I'd never written the stupid thing. I do love you, though, I do!'

'Oh darling,' Sarah laughed as she clasped me to her while Bob patted my back. 'We know you do. And we couldn't be prouder of you, honestly, darling. The essay is brilliant.'

I was officially the worst daughter in the world. I would buy a slab of granite and carve those words into it as I wandered the streets with it slung around my neck.

I clung to my mother and my father and they clung to me, and in that moment I knew they were weren't a bit bonkeresque. Well, just the tiniest bit, maybe. I would hardly be clinging to maddies, would I? No, I relied on these two forgiving 'rentals for everything. Scenes of uncountable kindnesses, angelic acts and selfless sacrifices

– all for a thankless daughter who hadn't even won her first international fencing tournament – montaged into one another.

My tears wouldn't stop no matter how many times they reassured me how proud they were of me.

Proud of *moi*?

Perhaps they *were* mad? I looked at my mother and then at Bob. They were quite fit for a couple of old folks in their early forties. My mother really needed to get something done with her hair, and Bob, well, his dress sense rivalled the chaviest wannabe hip-hop artist onstage. But with a visit to Saville Row for a few bespoke suit fittings, he really could make something of himself, I decided.

'I honestly didn't want to enter the competition, that part's true. But I did write those things, and now, well, you must hate me. Just a little bit?'

Bob and Sarah threw back their heads and laughed like an entire shop of old women's knickers.

THIRTY-FIVE

In Each Letter,
a Heart Beats

I returned to school on Sunday afternoon, and before dinner, every Year Eleven girl had gathered in my room. Some to offer their solidarity, some just out of curiosity. I was the cause celeb à la mode.

'I can't *believe* you'd dare to show your face after all the stories you sold about Calypso!' Star sniped at Honey as she cruised in with her fags.

Honey was equally outraged. 'Moi?' she asked, pointing to herself in shock. 'I was just trying to raise my dearest friend's profile a bit. I thought it only fair that someone tell *her* side of the story. Sorry for caring,' she added, slumping on my pillow.

'You gave them photographs of her drinking alcohol in a bar!' Portia pointed out. 'What sort of profile were you hoping to raise, exactly?'

Honey shrugged. 'Actually I thought it was a très flattering shot, considering I took it with my mobile.'

'How did Bob and Sarah take it?' Indie asked, looking at me with her chocolate brown eyes.

'They were absolutely amazing about everything.'

'What? Even about the essay?' Star probed.

I laughed. 'You know Bob. He thinks it was inevitable that his progeny would be a literary genius, and of course it's only natural that I used artistic licence.'

'I knew they'd support you, whatever you wrote,' Star reminded me, chucking me a Hershey's Kiss.

'I know. I guess I underestimated their capacity to worship all creative endeavours, no matter how rubbish it is.'

'I think you underestimate how much they care about you, actually. You've got the coolest 'rentals out of all of us,' Star insisted.

Everyone seemed to agree – even girls who'd never met Bob and Sarah.

'Listen, a part of me doesn't want to give you this, but, well, you probably should check out what he has to say,' Star told me as she chucked a letter from Freds at me.

It wasn't on palace paper, but I recognised the writing.

'It's from Freds,' I said as I opened it up. I looked at the eager faces of the girls gathered around me in the room. 'I'll read it later,' I said but Honey told everyone apart from my closest friends to leave. Actually, what she said was, 'Ciao, ciao, peasants.' Then she clapped her hands at them as if dispersing hens. Naturally, she stayed on and only about half the crew left, but I read the letter out anyway. I was too desperate to know the contents to hold on and too terrified to read it on my own.

Dear Calypso,

I'm not sure I should even be writing you this letter. Last time I wrote you a letter you went into a huge strop and accused The Palace of writing it. Well, I'm using school-headed paper this time, so unless you believe the dark conspiracy of The Palace extends to Eades, I hope you'll accept this letter is written in my own hand and take it in the spirit in which it's intended.

First up, BIG SORRY for the dumping by txt thing. I was totally out of order. Totally.

Secondly, BIG SORRY if you feel guilty about The Counter Dump thing. Don't! I deserved it. Billy told me about the whole scheme, but don't be too hard on him, he's a bit dopey in matters of love.

Thirdly (is thirdly even a word?) BIG SORRY for falling in the Thames and dragging your name through the mud in yet another media frenzy. See, this is why I didn't think I was right for you. You're mad and wild and well, I'm not. I'd like to be, but every time I do anything remotely out of the ordinary, like fall in the Thames, it's front-page news. That's probably why I'm such a boring git.

I also wanted you to know that I'm really happy that you and McHamish are hanging out. He gets you and I know you get him. It kills me that I will never be able to pull a girl as cool as you again. So I guess I'll have to stay confined to

my boring little box and face the fact that I will never be
enough for you. I wish I was wilder and cooler and capable
of being eccentric and worthy of a girl like you without a
media frenzy. But I'm not. You give good txt Calypso and I
know I've never laughed as much as when we were hanging
out.

Anyway, this letter is getting far too meaningful and
pathetic. A sad, tragic part of me even wants to say I hope
we can still be friends. (I hope you're not reading this out by
the way.)
Instead, let's just leave it as it is,
Laters,
Freds. xxx

I felt tears prickling my eyes as I folded the page up and
slipped it carefully back in the envelope. I would *definitely* be
hanging on to this letter, however tragic Star thought I was.

'I was wrong,' Star blurted, her eyes tearing up.

'What?'

I couldn't believe it, but her lip was actually wobbling.
'About Freds, I was wrong. You have soooo got to get back
with him.'

I shook my head. 'There is no way I am getting back
with him. The Counter Dump was the daftest idea ever. I
am so not –'

'No. I mean *really* back with him. He loves you. You
love him. I thought he was this up-himself boring git, but
he's not. He's nice and he's real and he's –'

'She's pulling Malcolm now,' Portia pointed out.

I didn't correct her because I couldn't bear to go through the whole Italian dumping drama – which I was fairly certain hadn't stuck anyway.

'Malcolm's balmy,' Star said, dismissing him with a flick of her strawberry-blonde locks.

'I like him,' I told her, even though my pulse was racing at what Star was saying about being wrong about Freds.

And besides, I *did* like Malcolm. The truth was I was already really missing him even though I was determined that he was too much of a drama for a drama queen like me.

'I like Malcolm too,' Star agreed. 'I like him more than Freds, actually, but that's not the point.'

'I think Calypso's right,' Indie added. 'She's with Malcolm now.'

'Me too,' Portia agreed, lifting her head from her magazine.

'Shame he doesn't play polo, really,' Fenella sighed. Her sister, Perdita, agreed.

'Well, if anyone is interested in *my* opinion,' Honey began, but she was wrestled to the ground and smothered in duvets by the entire room of girls.

Then my phone rang, and it was Malcolm. 'How's Rex?' he asked.

'Oh my God!' I exclaimed. 'I forgot all about Rex!' I said to the room at large.

'Who is Rex?' Star mouthed as everyone all around looked on confused.

'I'll call you back,' I told Malcolm, pressing End.

'I haven't even told you about Rex,' I told the room.

'Does Rex play polo?' Perdita asked, suddenly perking up with interest.

'Yaah, is he really, really fit?' Clemmie asked. 'I haven't pulled a boy for an age, and I think my lips may have atrophied,' she groaned, flopping backwards with the despair of it all.

Are all teenagers' lives as fearfully confusing as mine, I wondered as I began telling my *pazzo* tale of the Last Duckling.

THIRTY-SIX

Pulling the Past
in Pullers' Woods

Sisters Regina and Bethlehem had done a wonderful job of settling Rex into the convent. Actually, all the nuns adored Rex, and the feeling was mutual. They had the gardener build a small pond, and there was talk of finding him another little companion. Not that he was ever lonely. It was so adorable the way he followed Sister Regina around everywhere she went. I wondered if I could train Dorothy to do that. It would look soooo cool wandering around Windsor with a little bunny hopping along behind me.

The entire week was disrupted by journalists trying to get a personal account from me. But Sister Constance was by now only too familiar with the ways of the paparazzi, and they were thwarted at every attempt. All trips to Windsor were banned for the next weekend, but no one resented me too much for that, as the weather was so filthy. Also, Sunday night was the Burns Supper with the piping in of the pizza, and Star and Indie's band was performing *my* song, which I hadn't needed to rewrite once Indie attacked it with her thrashing guitar solo.

Malcolm called and sent the odd txt, but he was too busy editing *The Last Duckling* to give me much attention. The film was due to be screened the following Sunday at Eades, and Saint Augustine's was invited. I wondered what the film would be like, and okay, yes, I was also wondering if he'd get the chance to pull me. But mostly I was wondering about Freds – not whether he'd pull me, because his letter had made that pretty clear – but what it would be like to see him again. I had read and reread his letter so many times and agreed with Star that I at least needed to respond. What was the etiquette with royal ex-boyfriends?

I didn't see why it was so pathetic that we stay friends. I mean, we were bound to bump into one another, with our schools being so close and both of us being on our school's sabre teams.

Five drafts of my reply later, I decided to txt him and see if he wanted to meet up in Pullers' Woods for a chat. Pullers' Woods seemed like a good place, with the paps still lurking all over Windsor and outside the perimeter of the razor wire.

Freds replied immediately.

Sun a/noon, by tree that attack dog chased you up? F

I replied:

C U there, C

I tried not to dwell on the fact that we weren't doing x's anymore. I decided to take Rex to meet Freds. I needed the support, and also I thought it might break the ice to have a third party there, and I didn't trust Star not to hiss instructions to me.

It was snowing, so I had to wrap Rex in a rug, which Sister Bethlehem had crocheted five hundred years ago and smelt of mothballs. The smell made me sneeze the whole way through the woods. The snow was falling lightly, but not many flakes were making it through the bare branches of the trees. Everything felt still and magical, and I half expected a lion to wander out and start chatting to me. I was armed with Honey's mace in the event we ran into any attack dogs who might be in the mood to eat ducklings, but none came my way.

I had dressed carefully in jeans and a hoodie so Freds didn't think I was making an effort. I'd also taken special care to only wear lots of lip-gloss and mascara, for that no-makeup look that boys love. Careless and carefree was the note I was hoping to strike.

Freds was already there, by the tree, as arranged. Punctual as ever. His hair wasn't doing that sticky-outy thing I loved so much, although now that I knew about his covert gel usage, I was not as enamoured of his hair as I used to be. He'd had it cut, and he looked vulnerable rather than cool, but, oh my God, he was still heartbreakingly fit. It must be the prince thing.

'H-Hi,' I stuttered awkwardly. 'Erm, this is Rex. I thought you might want to meet him because, well, he's the star of the film Malcolm shot in Florence, and well, you'll be seeing it next Sunday. He's very excited. Rex, I mean. Although Malcolm's obviously feverishly excited too. I mean, it's his film,' I blurted.

Freds laughed. I couldn't tell if he was laughing because I was mad as a drawer of old ladies' knickers or because he thought I was funny.

Freds stroked Rex on the beak and Rex nipped Fred's finger. It was all very touching. Then Freds took him out of his swaddling blanket and placed him on the snow and Rex went bonkeresque. He started nipping the snow and dashing about trying to catch flakes as they fell. His little webbed prints looked soooo adorable in the snow.

Freds and I watched him running about like a mad thing for a bit and then we looked at one another. And then Freds kissed me. First on the forehead and then on the nose.

Then just as I feared (or was it a longing?), he was about to kiss my lips, but he said, 'I'm going to the States in the Easter holidays.'

'Cool. Me too,' I said. I mean, I live in America, and Bob and Sarah were going back with me then. And of course, Freds knew all that. Freds knew everything.

'I'm doing this tour thing with Gran and the 'rents.'

'Fancy that,' I replied. I know, I know! I can't believe I said that. The spirit of my own gran must have inhabited my brain.

Freds didn't seem a bit fazed by my insanity, though. 'Yaah, so, the thing is, I know I said it was pathetic to want to be friends, but well . . . I wondered if I might see you there?'

'Where?' I asked, because I was still mentally kicking myself for saying 'fancy that!'

I closed my eyes to gather my thoughts, and that was when he did it. That was when he really kissed me, on the mouth – with his lips. And while it was most *tranquillo* and *fantastico* and *molto* gorgeous, I pulled away.

Then my phone rang. It was Malcolm, and my heart skipped a beat. Not because Freds had just attempted to pull me, but because I realised that I really wanted to see Malcolm more than anyone else in the world. 'It's Malcolm,' I whispered to Freds, as I pressed Answer.

'Want to meet up in Pullers' Woods in a bit?' Malcolm asked. 'So you can dump me again?'

I giggled. 'Sure, I'll bring Rex for a visit. Call me when you're almost there,' I told him, totally longing to see him.

'I'm almost there, actually,' he said. 'Just through the barbed wire gap now.'

'Well, hurry up, then, I'm already here! So's Freds,' I told him, because I didn't want any subterfuge between us. Apart from not wanting to muck Malcolm around, he was the sort of person I could be honest with and be myself around.

'Cool,' he replied happily. 'See you in a mo.'

Freddie, on the other hand, looked at me with one of his wretched disappointed looks.

I poked out my tongue and then – shock, horror – HRH poked *his* tongue out at me!

'Sorry,' Freds said, rubbing his long, tapered fingers through his hair. 'About the kiss thing earlier. I didn't mean for that to happen.'

'It's okay,' I told him gently, suddenly maddeningly aware of his lemony smell again. 'It's just not right. Not now,' I told him maturely even though my mind was screaming, HAVE ONE LAST KISS! HE'S THE PRINCE, YOU MADDY!

Oh, buggery bollocks, just when I thought I knew what I felt, and whom I felt *it* for.

Princes! You can't live with them, but then again, can you really live without them?

Calypso's fencing terms and English words

FENCING TERMS

attack *au fer*: an attack that is prepared by deflecting an opponent's blade

bout: one single fight, usually lasting around six minutes

disengagement: a way to continue attacking after being parried

en garde: the 'ready' position fencers take before play

épée: another weapon used in fencing

parry: defensive move, a block

piste: a fourteen-metre-long combat area on which a bout is fought

point: the tip of a weapon's blade

pool: a group into which fencers are divided during preliminary rounds to assess ranking

retire: retreat

riposte: an offensive action made immediately after a parry of the opponent's attack

sabre: The only cutting fencing blade. Points are scored both by hits made with the tip of the blade and by cuts made with the blade, but more commonly by cuts. The sabre target is everything above the leg, including the head and arms. For this reason the entire weapon, including the guard, registers hits on an electrical apparatus even though hitting the weapon's guard is not legal. This means the sabreur is totally wired – unlike fencers using the other weapons. Before play begins, the sabreurs must check that all parts of their electric kit are working. This is done by the sabreurs tapping their opponents on the mask, the sabre, the guard and the metal jacket so that all hits will be recorded

salle: fencing hall or club

salute: once formal, now a casual acknowledgement of one's opponent and president at the start of a bout

seeding: the process of eliminating fencers from their pools, based on the results of their bouts

trompement: deception of the parry

ENGLISH WORDS

arse: *derrière.* To make an arse of yourself means to embarrass yourself

ASBO: Anti-Social Behaviour Order; a punishment handed out to youth who graffiti or get drunk or use foul language

blag: to talk your way into or out of something, or to fake something

bless: an affectionate, sweet exclamation, but like all English words, it can be used sarcastically

blank/to be blanked: to not register someone; to look through them

blue: blue paper given to write lines on; a minor punishment

bollocks: literally means testicles but used to mean useless, nonsense, ridiculous

bottle out: chicken out, lose your nerve. 'Bottle' is another word for 'nerve,' so you can also 'lose your bottle'

chav/chavie: A person defined by a common way of behaving or dressing. They have their favourite designer brands and love loads of bling. The opposite of posh or Sloaney

common: slang for vulgar, of low social status, lacking charm or manners. Note: you can be rich and still be common

cut: to ignore someone, to look right through them; see *blank*

Daddy's plastic: parental credit cards

DPGs: Daddy's Plastic Girls; girls who are defined by their limitless credit card privileges

dressing down: telling off

en suite: bathroom attached to bedroom

exeat: weekend at which pupils attending boarding school go home, usually every three weeks

extract the urine: a polite way of saying 'take the piss'

fag: cigarette

fancy (v): to find someone attractive

Febreze: spray used to remove odours from clothes

fit: cute, hot, attractive. Girls and boys both use the word to describe the opposite sex. Note: a girl wouldn't refer to another girl as fit – she'd say 'stunning'

gating: a punishment in which one is not permitted to leave the school grounds on weekends

hoodie: sweatshirt with a hood

house mother or house mistress: female head of a boarding house

It Girl: a society girl of royal extraction with a large media profile

Kiltland: Scotland

kit: equipment and outfit for specific event or activity

knickers: panties

leg it: make a run for it

mad: eccentric, crazy or unreasonable – out there

madly: very, as in 'madly late'

mobile: cell phone

Old Chokey: a prison

pash: pashmina

piss-take/to take the piss: to tease, mimic or to make fun of someone, either maliciously or fondly; a joke (see *extract the urine*, above)

pleb: short for plebeian – a derogatory term suggesting lack of class

plebbie: (adj) for pleb (see above)

point: as in making a point in an argument

prat: idiot, fool

pull: to make out, score, kiss, etc.

public school: exclusive boarding school

rinse: to totally decimate your opponent in sport or debate

rip: to ridicule, tease; equivalent to 'take the piss'

Sloane: posh, snooty girl (named after Sloane Street and Square, an upscale area in London)

snog-age: (rhymes with 'corsage') to tongue kiss

sorted: an expression of approval; 'no problem'

soz: sorry

spliff: marijuana; a joint

tomoz: tomorrow

taking the piss: to tease someone, rip it out of them, see *piss-take*

term: Three terms make up a school year: winter term is before Christmas; spring term is between Christmas and Easter; summer term is between Easter and the summer holiday

toff: snobby aristocrat

tuck: snack foods you are allowed to bring to boarding school; junk food

tuck in: pig out

wardrobe: closet

wind up: to tease either gently or nastily

Year: girls start boarding at age 11 in Year Seven, and the 'Years' go up to Year Eleven (ages 15–16). The final two years are referred to as the Lower Sixth and Upper Sixth (ages 16–17 and 18, respectively)

Cisco@thecontradictions.com

Tyne O'Connell

is the author of the Calypso Chronicles series—
Pulling Princes, Stealing Princes, Dueling Princes
and *Dumping Princes*—as well as *True Love, the
Sphinx, and Other Unsolvable Riddles* and several
adult comedy fiction books. She always fancied
herself a bit of a fencer, but mostly she just fancied
the boys who fenced. Tyne lives in Mayfair,
London, pining for her daughter to come home
from boarding school so they can shop and gossip.

www.calypsochronicles.com